SPECIAL EDITION JUNIOR NOVELIZATION

randomhousekids.com

ISBN 978-0-553-53690-4 (hc) — ISBN 978-0-553-53691-1 (ebook)

Printed in the United States of America

10 9 8 7 6 5 4 3

SPECIAL EDITION JUNIOR NOVELIZATION

PEACHTREE

A novelization by David Lewman

Based on the Story by Rick Jaffa & Amanda Silver
and the Screenplay by Rick Jaffa & Amanda Silver
and Derek Connolly & Colin Trevorrow
and characters created by Michael Crichton

Random House 🏠 New York

Chapter One

Gray Mitchell was in his bedroom, clicking through 3-D images on his red plastic View-Master®. His parents had given him three disks with dinosaur pictures for his fifth birthday. That meant he'd been looking at these same pictures for six years.

In kid years, that made the disks prehistoric, but he still liked them.

He also liked his model of two dinosaurs fighting on a volcanic island. And his dinosaur posters. And his books about dinosaurs. In fact, Gray liked *anything* to do with dinosaurs. Well, not liked. Loved.

And now he was finally going to get to see some real ones! *Real, live, moving, chomping, stomping dinosaurs!* He wanted to be ready. He wanted to remember everything he knew about dinosaurs when he finally got to meet them face to face.

"Gray?" his mom asked, opening his door. "Let's

move. Why are you looking at that now, honey? Grab your backpack. The flight's in two hours."

He kept peering into his View-Master®. "Dane County Airport is thirty-eight minutes away. Sixty with traffic." Gray was very good with numbers.

Dane County Airport served Gray's hometown of Madison, Wisconsin. There weren't a lot of live dinosaurs in Wisconsin. In fact, there were none. Nada. Zilch.

"How many minutes to get your little butt in the van?" his mom asked. "Move, kiddo."

Gray put the View-Master® in an outer pocket of his backpack, pulled on the pack, and followed his mom out to their minivan parked in the driveway. His dad was waiting in the driver's seat. "Zach!" he called out the car window. "Vamonos!"

Zach, Gray's sixteen-year-old brother, was standing in the yard, touching his forehead to his girlfriend's forehead. She was in love with Zach. Zach liked her but wasn't really sure he loved her.

"Call me every day," his girlfriend said, close to tears. "And text me pictures so I don't forget what you look like."

"I'll only be gone for a week," Zach said sheepishly.

His dad called from the car again. "Zach, you're not being sent off to war here."

At the same moment that Zach's girlfriend said, "I love you," Zach said, "I'll see you later. Bye." He climbed into the backseat of the minivan, watching his girlfriend wave. She was trying not to cry, but it looked as though she was going to anyway.

Zach's mom turned around and said, "I know it hurts, sweetheart." But his dad didn't believe Zach's relationship with his girlfriend was serious. "Are you . . . are you going to be . . . okay?" he asked, teasing.

Zach blew out a big breath. He couldn't decide which was more annoying: his dad's teasing or his mom's sympathy. He stuck in his earbuds, retreating into his music.

His mom glared at his dad as he started the car and began the trip to the airport.

Just outside the security checkpoint, the two brothers said goodbye to their parents. Gray's mom knelt to hug him as he adjusted his waterproof fanny pack. It was filled with everything he thought he might need for his adventure with *real* dinosaurs.

"Passengers must be at the gate thirty minutes before departure," he said. Gray hated being late. And there was no way he was going to miss *this* plane.

"I know, honey," his mom said. She stood up, turned to Zach, and took his face in her hands. "Watch your brother," she instructed. "And answer your phone. I didn't turn on international roaming so you could snaptalk or whatever you call it."

Their dad put his hand on Zach's shoulder. "Listen to your mother," he said in mock seriousness.

Zach nodded his head and rolled his eyes at the same time. Then the boys said goodbye and hurried through security. Their mom watched them disappear into the crowd. "I love you!" she called after them.

"Did you call your sister?" Dad asked her.

Mom nodded. "Yes, but my call went straight to voice-mail. She never answers."

"It'll be fine," Dad reassured her. "She handles twenty thousand people a day. She can handle two more."

Hours later, the plane landed in Costa Rica. As the two brothers got off the plane, they saw signs directing them to the ferry for Isla Nublar.

As they shuffled up the gangway to the ferry with the other tourists, Gray asked, "How big is the island?"

Zach shrugged. He really had no idea, but he wasn't going to admit that to his little brother. "Big."

"But how many pounds?" Gray asked.

Zach made a face. "That doesn't make sense."

Once they were on the sleek ferry, it sped across the ocean waves toward Isla Nublar. Gray was so excited, he was bouncing. Zach noticed a cute teenage girl and put a little distance between himself and his brother. Gray noticed but didn't stop bouncing.

In the distance, the island rose out of the sea. It had mountains that looked as though they might have once been volcanoes. And it was green, covered in dense jungle.

But Isla Nublar had much more than just mountains and jungle. It was home to the number one tourist destination in the world, where visitors could experience the thrill of witnessing living and breathing dinosaurs! And even though he would never admit it, Zach was almost as excited as Gray was to be on this trip.

When the ferry reached the island, Zach and Gray made their way off the boat with the crowd of tourists. They scanned the landing, looking for their aunt.

She wasn't there.

Instead, her assistant, Zara, a young woman in her

twenties, stood waiting for them, holding up a tablet that read "Zach and Gray Mitchell."

"Where's Aunt Claire?" Gray asked his brother.

Zach shrugged. They ambled toward Zara, who introduced herself and led them onto the monorail.

Gray made his way down the aisle, gently squeezing between people to reach the front. The front of the monorail was glass, so whoever stood there saw everything first.

Gray reached the front window, pressed his hands to the glass, and watched as the monorail swooshed along on its elevated rails, passing through the jungle foliage on either side.

And then he saw it.

A huge gate with burning torches loomed in front of them. The top of the gate read "Jurassic World." The monorail passed through the open gate, and they were officially inside the park.

The monorail took them right to the hotel. Gray raced out into the busy lobby, feeling as though he were about to burst. Zach followed behind his brother with Zara, who pulled both of their rolling bags. Zara spoke in her crisp British accent. "Your aunt arranged to greet you at one o'clock. Could your brother slow down?"

"He doesn't slow down," Zach explained.

From halfway up the escalator, Gray waved back to them.

When they reached their hotel room, Gray ran inside. "Let's-go-let's-go-*let's-go*!"

"Dude," Zach said, trying to calm him down. "She said we have to wait."

"I don't want to wait anymore!"

Gray ran to the room's balcony and threw open the door. . . .

Chapter Two

What a view! The park was beautiful and exciting—everything Gray had hoped it would be. From their balcony, he could see the lagoon, the visitors' center, Main Street . . .

. . . everything but dinosaurs.

"When can we go see the dinosaurs?" Gray asked Zara.

"After you meet up with your aunt Claire in the visitors' center," Zara said. "At one o'clock. As I mentioned."

Gray looked disappointed. He wanted to see the dinosaurs *now*.

But at that moment, Gray and Zach's aunt Claire was busy doing her job. As an important executive of Jurassic World, she was giving a tour to three businesspeople she hoped would invest in the park. She led them through sliding glass doors of the Genetics Lab into a long glass corridor packed with tourists. Here the visitors could watch the park's scientists at work.

"No one's impressed by a dinosaur anymore," Claire said, smiling. "Twenty years ago, de-extinction was right up there with magic. These days, kids look at a *Stegosaurus* like an elephant at the city zoo."

Inside the lab, dinosaur eggs warmed in incubators. A baby *Apatosaurus* broke through its shell. Children pressed against the glass wall of the corridor, staring. Despite what Claire had said, they seemed fascinated by the newborn dinosaur.

"That doesn't mean Asset Development is falling behind," Claire continued as she led her three visitors through the hall. "Our DNA excavators discover new species every year. But consumers want them bigger, louder. More teeth."

She led the trio into the Genetics Lab. The scientists were drilling into amber to extract ancient DNA, injecting fertilized eggs, and loading stacks of frozen embryos into freezers. "The good news," she said, "is that our advances in gene splicing have opened up a new frontier. We've learned more from genetics in the past decade than in a century of digging up bones."

Stopping before a 3-D display of a strand of DNA,

she asked the businesspeople, "When you say you want to sponsor a new attraction, what do you have in mind?"

One man smiled. "We want to be thrilled."

Claire smiled back. "Don't we all."

She swiped the touchscreen glass of the display case, and the DNA strand spun. "We think you'll be more than thrilled by our first genetically modified hybrid, *Indominus rex*. A new species of dinosaur, built from scratch."

"And not just built," a nearby voice said. "Designed."

The group turned and saw Dr. Henry Wu, the genetic scientist who worked for Jurassic World, and Jurassic Park before it. He had been there from the beginning.

"She'll be fifty feet long when fully grown," Dr. Wu continued. "Bigger than the *T. rex.*"

The three potential corporate sponsors looked intrigued, but not entirely sold. Claire said, "Every time we've unveiled a new asset, attendance at the park has spiked. We've gotten global news coverage. Celebrity visitors. Eyes of the world."

She knew that was the sort of thing corporate sponsors loved to hear.

"When will she be ready?" the woman in the group asked.

Like a predator sensing an easy kill, Claire smiled. "She already is."

Before she met her nephews at the visitors' center, Claire stopped by the park's control room. A couple dozen employees were watching the park on monitors.

Lowery, an engineer, knew she'd been meeting with potential corporate sponsors. "Did you close the deal?"

"I did," Claire said. Lowery shook his head. He clearly disapproved. "Why stop there? Might as well let the corporations *name* the dinosaurs! Just like the ballparks."

Valerie, a communications operator, answered a phone and said, "Your assistant is on line two. Zach and Gray are here."

"Tell her I'll be there in five," Claire said. She noticed Lowery's curious look. "My sister's kids."

"You're related to people? Actual human beings?" Lowery asked mockingly.

"Funny," Claire said, not amused, as she walked briskly out of the lab.

Chapter Three

Gray ran up the steps of the towering visitors' center. "This is it! Hurry up!"

Zach lagged behind. "Dude, chill."

Chilling was not on Gray's agenda. He slipped through the glass doors into the visitors' center and looked up. A skeleton of a *T. rex* petrified in a column of amber loomed over the hall. The monorail sliced through the open space above it.

In a 3-D display, a character named Mr. DNA explained the park's invisible fence system. "With our new invisible fence technology, the dinosaurs can stay in designated zones without bars or cages!"

An animated *Stegosaurus* approached a red line. A light around his neck flashed. He stopped and backed off.

Gray ran up to a display called "A Brief History of Neo-Paleontology." A genetic sequence scrolled by rapidly. Gray said, "Cytosine, guanine, adenine, and thymine.

The same four things writing the code for everything that ever lived—"

Zach caught up with Gray and grabbed him. "If you get lost, I'm not looking for you. Mom and Dad aren't paying me for babysitting."

Babysitting? That hurt.

"Gray?" asked a voice behind them. "Is that you?"

They turned around and saw their aunt Claire, kneeling, holding her arms open awkwardly. "Aunt Claire!" Gray said happily, running in for a hug. She stood up and faced Zach. "Wow, Zach, the last time I saw you, you were"—she held her hand out, indicating a height even shorter than Gray—"that must have been, what . . . three, four years ago?"

"Seven," Zach said. "Close."

Ouch, Claire thought. But she smiled and said, "So you got your VIP passes. And these are for food." She handed Zach an envelope. "Zara is going to take good care of you until I'm done working, okay?"

Gray was disappointed. "You're not coming with us?"

Claire's phone buzzed. "I wish I could," she said, feeling guilty. "But tomorrow I can take you into the control room and show you what goes on behind the scenes. That'd be cool, right?"

Zach and Gray nodded, looking abandoned.

"Okay," Claire said, smiling. "I'll see you tonight at six."

"Don't forget the thing with——" Zara reminded her boss.

"Eight," Claire corrected. "What time do you go to sleep? Or do you go to sleep at different times?"

She looked at her phone. The text read, "BOSS COMING."

"Right. Have fun," Claire said to her nephews. She turned to Zara and said, "Take care of them, okay?" Then she walked off quickly, leaving the boys alone with her assistant.

On the park's helipad, a helicopter labeled Jurassic One landed. Her hair whipped by the wind from the chopper's blades, Claire ran up to the door in her high-heeled shoes and climbed in. At the controls sat Simon Masrani, the billionaire who was Jurassic World's biggest investor. Next to him was a weary flight instructor.

"Claire!" Masrani shouted, greeting her over the noise of the helicopter.

"Mr. Masrani!" Claire shouted back. "You're flying?"

"I got my license!" he announced, grinning. But the

flight instructor shook his head. "Well," Masrani admitted, "almost. I only have to pass two more tests. Now show me my new dinosaur!"

He moved the controls. The helicopter lifted off the pad but spun around in a circle. Claire gripped a strap tightly. Masrani sucked his teeth. "Got it! Got it!"

They soared over the valley. Claire opened a notebook to a drawing of the new dinosaur's home, a steel paddock in the jungle. "So the marketing department thought we could offset costs by selling naming rights to the new paddock. I just closed a deal this morning—"

"Enough about costs," Masrani interrupted. "Don't forget why we built this place, Claire. Jurassic World exists to remind us how very small we are. How new. You can't put a price on that. Now, please! We're flying! Breathe!"

Claire tried to breathe as the helicopter veered around the curve of a mountaintop. Below, a steel structure stuck out of the jungle.

The home of the *Indominus rex*.

Chapter Four

Masrani landed the helicopter next to a massive, open-roofed steel paddock still under construction. The flying instructor jumped out of the chopper and ran to the nearest bushes. Claire heard retching sounds.

"Is he okay?" she asked.

"He's just being dramatic," Masrani claimed.

The billionaire noticed construction workers adding concrete extensions onto the paddock's massive walls. "We're still building?"

"We'd planned to open in May," Claire explained, "but Asset Containment insisted we build the walls up higher. It's bigger than they expected."

Masrani smiled. "They had to build a bigger crib for me when I was a child. It's a good sign."

Claire led Masrani into an area encased in thick glass. Paddock supervisors monitored infrared displays. The red outline of a large animal could be seen on a monitor.

"We hit a few speed bumps early on," Claire said. "It began to anticipate where the food would come from. One of the handlers nearly lost an arm. The others threatened to quit if I couldn't guarantee their safety."

Masrani looked more impressed than concerned. "Anticipating where the food'll come from—so she's intelligent."

"For a dinosaur," Claire said.

Masrani noticed spiderweb cracks in the glass. "And that?"

"It tried to break the glass," Claire explained.

"I like her spirit," Masrani said, grinning.

They watched as workers lowered a full side of beef into the paddock on a chain. Masrani, eager to get his first glimpse of the hybrid dinosaur, waited for *Indominus rex* to take its food. A palm frond rustled. Then . . . *WHOOM!* A clawed reptilian hand swept the side of beef into the foliage. As the dinosaur devoured the huge hunk of meat, Masrani got a glimpse of her muscular back. It was grayish white, with sharp bumps running down the spine.

"It's white!" Masrani said, delighted. "You never told me it's white!"

"Think it will scare the kids?" Claire asked.

"The kids?" Masrani said. "This will give the *parents* nightmares."

"Is that good?" Claire asked, looking doubtful.

"It's fantastic!" Masrani said, stepping closer to the glass. "People will hate this animal . . . and they will love it."

As if the creature knew it was being discussed, the *Indominus rex* whipped its head around, looking over its shoulder directly at Claire and Masrani. Though its face was partially obscured by trees, its red eye was clearly visible, staring with malice.

Claire took a step back, unnerved by the look in the *Indominus*'s eye.

"Can she see us?" Masrani asked.

"They say it can sense thermal radiation," Claire said. "Like snakes."

The gigantic dinosaur kept staring in their direction, as though it was trying to figure out exactly where they were.

"I thought there were two of them," Masrani said.

"There was a sibling in case this one didn't survive infancy."

"Where's the sibling?"

"She ate it."

THUNK! The skeleton of the butchered side of beef hit the ground, picked clean by the dinosaur. Masrani gulped. "So this paddock is quite safe, then?"

"We have the best structural engineers in the world," Claire said confidently.

"Mm-hmm," Masrani said, sounding unconvinced. An idea occurred to him. "There's an American Navy man on the island. Part of a research program one of my companies is running. Owen Grady."

Claire didn't hide the fact that she wasn't thrilled to hear this name. "I know who he is."

Masrani didn't notice Claire's reaction. "His animals often try to escape. They're smart, so he has to be smarter."

"He only thinks he's smarter."

Masrani eyed Claire, sensing some history between her and Owen Grady. Unfazed, he pressed on with his idea. "I want you to bring him in. Let him inspect the paddock. Maybe he can see something we can't."

Claire frowned. But when Masrani looked at her, she was nodding.

On another part of the island, in the Raptor Research

Area, a pig was running for its life. *BAM!* The pig ran right into a steel wall. It squealed.

It had a good reason to squeal. In fact, it had four.

Four *Velociraptors* stared at the pig. They crouched, ready to pounce.

But a whistle stopped them cold. They looked up. Owen Grady stood on a metal catwalk above them, holding his hand flat like a military command.

The lead *Velociraptor* turned its bright yellow eyes back toward the cowering pig and lashed toward it.

Another sharp whistle.

"Watch it, Blue," Owen warned.

Blue stepped back into formation with the other three *Velociraptors*. The green-and-black *Velociraptor* next to her screeched up at Owen.

"Don't give me that, Charlie," Owen told the dinosaur. He closed his hand into a fist, releasing the *Velociraptors*. They disappeared back into the foliage, leaving the pig alone.

The other employees whooped and clapped. The lead *Velociraptor* handler, Barry, slapped Owen on the back, congratulating him. "You finally did it, man!"

"Only eighty dead pigs ain't bad, right?" Owen said.

"And this pig will love you for the rest of your life," Barry said.

As they climbed down from the metal catwalk, a slightly older man in a suit marched up to them. "Owen! Heckuva job, buddy!"

Owen was not excited to see Vic Hoskins. . . .

Chapter Five

Technically, Hoskins was Owen's boss. He'd hired him to work for InGen, the company in charge of the *Velociraptor* research program.

But that didn't mean Owen had to like him.

Hoskins smiled. "I was starting to think I'd hired the wrong guy, but you got those dinosaurs eating out of your palm!"

Owen shrugged. "You came on a good day. It's not usually a happy ending."

"Is that why you haven't been sending in reports?"

"We've been busy."

"Not too busy to cash your paychecks."

Owen brushed past Hoskins, but the older man followed him. "What do you want, Hoskins?"

"A field test," Hoskins answered. "You've proven the *Velociraptors* will respond to commands. Let's put this research on its feet."

Owen kept walking. "These are wild animals. Trust me—you don't want them in the field."

"I just saw a bond—a real bond—between man and beast." Hoskins cut in front of Owen, blocking him.

"You're in my way," Owen said.

Hoskins didn't budge. "Come on, man. You and I? We're dogs of war. The military's looking to reduce casualties. Most people would tell you robots are the future. But nature already gave us the most effective killing machines seventy-five million years ago! And now we know they can take orders!"

Barry had caught up with them and heard Hoskins's speech. "We finally make progress and that's the first thing he says? Make a weapon?"

Hoskins held both hands up. "Come on, gents. These *Velociraptors* have millions of years of instinct in their cells. Instinct we can program. Their loyalty can't be bought. They'll charge right into the enemy's teeth and eat 'em, belt buckles and all!"

"And what if they decide they want to be in control?" Barry asked.

Hoskins shrugged. "Remind 'em who *is* in control. Terminate the rogues, and promote only the loyal bloodlines."

Owen shook his head. "You come in here. You don't learn anything about them except what you want to know. You made them, and now you think you own them."

Hoskins looked surprised. "We *do* own them. An extinct animal doesn't have any rights."

"They're not extinct anymore," Owen countered.

"Exactly," Hoskins agreed. "We're sitting on a gold mine, and Masrani's using it to stock a petting zoo."

"He's trying to teach people some humility," Owen said. "He doesn't make weapons." He faked left, then slipped past Hoskins on the right. Hoskins kept following him, grinning slightly.

"You think the eighth-richest man in the world is only into oil, telecom, and family fun parks?" he asked. "Masrani's so diversified, he doesn't even know *what* he owns!"

Owen realized Hoskins was serious. "How long has InGen been planning to sell this idea of using the *Velociraptors* as weapons?"

"Since the day we hired you out of the Navy," Hoskins answered. "Those animals could take the place of thousands of boots on the ground. How many lives would that save?"

Owen closed the metal gate behind him. It locked

automatically, leaving Hoskins on the other side. But he kept talking.

"Look around you, Owen. Every living thing in this jungle is trying to murder the other. It's the way Mother Nature refines the pecking order. War is struggle. Struggle breeds greatness. Without that, we end up with places like this, charging seven bucks for a soda."

Barry couldn't believe it. "Can you hear yourself when you talk?"

"This will happen with or without you," Hoskins said. "Progress always wins."

"Maybe progress should lose for a change," Owen said.

In the *Velociraptor* enclosure, a young handler dropped a loop around the pig. Suddenly the pig bolted, pulling the handler into the arena! "Man down in the pen!" Barry yelled.

The squealing pig ran into the bushes, where the raptors made quick work of it. Then they emerged into the open area, walking directly toward the young handler. He scrambled on the ground, backing away from the approaching *Velociraptors*.

They moved closer. . . .

Chapter Six

Three armed Jurassic World troopers aimed their electric rifles at the *Velociraptors*. "Targeting raptors Blue, Charlie, Delta, Echo," one of them barked.

"Hold your fire!"

Owen raced back onto the catwalk and dropped down between the raptors and the fallen handler.

"Owen, no!" Barry cried.

The troopers froze. They couldn't believe what Owen had just done.

Owen raised his hand and approached Blue. "Put twelve amps in these animals, and they'll never trust me again!"

Hoskins watched, fascinated.

"Stand down, Blue," Owen ordered. "Stand down, girl." Delta snapped her jaws. "Hey! What did I say?"

Blue snapped at Delta, bringing her back into line. Owen stepped forward, within inches of Blue, and signaled to the raptors with his other hand.

They backed off.

"Open the gate," Owen said without taking his eyes off the *Velociraptors*.

When the handlers hesitated, the guy who'd fallen in the pen yelled, "Open the gate!"

The heavy gate opened. The young handler slid out beneath it. Owen slowly backed up and rolled under the gate as it fell shut.

Owen coughed on the dust. Barry offered him his hand. "You're crazy! You know that?"

Once he was standing, Owen extended a hand to the young guy and lifted him off the ground. "You're new, huh? Ever wonder why there was a job opening?"

The young guy's eyes widened.

"And never stand with your back to the cage," Owen added. The young guy looked over his shoulder and saw Charlie, the raptor, right on the other side of the bars, with her mouth open wide.

In the park's Gentle Giants Petting Zoo, Gray snapped pictures of a young *Triceratops*. Zach shook his head. "This place is for little kids."

"Yeah, I know," Gray said. "Wanna go on the spinning

dinosaur eggs?"

Shaking his head, Zach looked over at Zara, talking on her cell phone. She was paying no attention to the brothers. Zach got a glint in his eye. "Scatter," he said to Gray.

"Huh?"

"Run! Go!"

The two brothers raced out of the petting zoo, ditching Zara. She was so busy talking on her phone, she didn't even notice.

On Main Street, the boys weaved through the crowd. Zach checked back over his shoulder. Gray spotted a massive paddock and ran toward it. *"T. rex! T. rex! T. rex!"*

Inside the T. Rex Kingdom, the boys saw a grove of redwood trees and a live goat on a platform. They made their way into the fake fallen tree where tourists were waiting to see the *T. rex*.

A park employee, high in a crow's nest, cracked a flare and tossed it at the goat, hoping to attract the *T. rex*'s attention.

It worked.

Suddenly the enormous *T. rex* burst out of the grove of redwoods, grabbed the goat, and devoured it.

Gray felt sorry for the goat . . . but he loved seeing the *T. rex*! This was more like it!

Owen returned to the simple wooden bungalow he'd built in a corner of the lagoon. The bungalow was attached to a silver Airstream camper with solar panels.

He got to work on his vintage motorcycle, trying to put Hoskins and his ideas about dinosaur weapons out of his mind.

But his solitude didn't last long. A Mercedes drove toward his place, kicking up dust. "What do they want now?" he wondered.

Claire got out of the car. She strode across the uneven ground in her high heels. "Mr. Grady? Can I have a moment? I need you to come take a look at something."

Owen looked puzzled. "Why are you calling me Mr. Grady?"

"Owen," Claire said reluctantly. "We have a dinosaur— a new species we've made."

Owen raised his eyebrows. "You just went and *made* a new dinosaur?"

"Yes. It's kind of what we do here," Claire said, exasperated. "The exhibit opens to the public in three weeks.

Mr. Masrani wanted me to consult with you."

Owen kept working on his motorcycle. He tossed a loose bolt in Claire's direction. She jumped away when it hit the ground near her. "Why me?" Owen asked.

Claire was wondering the same thing, but she said, "I guess Mr. Masrani thinks since you're able to control the raptors, you might have insight into this asset—"

"Asset?" Owen said, sneering as he wiped grease off his hands. "You're in charge of all these animals, but you don't even act like they're alive."

"I'm fully aware they're alive," Claire said coldly.

"They're not numbers on a spreadsheet," Owen continued. "You may have made them in a test tube, but they don't know that."

Claire didn't like being lectured by this . . . animal trainer. She turned to walk back to her car but stumbled in her high heels. Owen caught her.

"You might want to change your shirt," she told him, wrinkling her nose. "They're very sensitive to smell."

She pulled free of his grasp and strode back to her car. On the back of her suit were palm prints from Owen's greasy hands.

Shaking his head, Owen followed her.

Chapter Seven

From the *T. rex* paddock, Gray and Zach had hurried to see the *Mosasaurus* feeding show in the lagoon. They made their way past droves of tourists, looking for two empty seats in the bleachers along the water's edge.

Over a loudspeaker, an announcer was saying, "The *Mosasaurus* is thought to have hunted near the surface of the water, where it preyed on anything it could sink its teeth into—turtles, large fish, even smaller mosasaurs."

But the crowd wasn't really listening. Their attention was fixed on a huge shark, suspended in the air on a cable. The shark carcass was moving into position over the center of the lagoon.

The shark was a snack.

"Okay, folks, let's see if she's still hungry after already eating today," the announcer said in a cheerful voice. "She's a little shy, so be nice and give her a hand when she comes out."

Zach stared at his phone, texting. Gray tapped his arm. "Zach. *Mosasaurus.* Zach!"

An enormous swell formed in the water. The crowd rose to their feet.

Zach looked at a photo of his girlfriend holding a "MISS YOU" sign.

"ZACH!" Gray said insistently. "You're missing it!"

Zach looked up through a forest of raised cell phones just in time to see—

The *Mosasaurus* exploded straight up out of the water! It grabbed the shark in its massive jaws!

The crowd gasped. The huge aquatic reptile crashed back into the water, soaking the crowd with a gigantic wave! People screamed and laughed.

Zach and Gray looked at each other in disbelief. Then they burst into laughter.

"It was fifty-five feet long!" Gray shouted.

BZZZZKK! The bleachers automatically lowered so the audience could see the *Mosasaurus* under the water, devouring the shark. It finished eating in only a few terrible gulps. With a whip of its tail, the beast disappeared into the dark-blue depths.

"That," Zach admitted, "was pretty good."

"It had eighty-eight teeth!" Gray said.

Zach laughed. He stuck his phone in his pocket. "Want to see something else cool?"

At the *Indominus rex* paddock, Owen stared out the window of the observation tower. "What's this hybrid dinosaur made of?"

"The base genome is *T. rex*," Claire said. "The rest is classified."

"You made a new dinosaur, and you don't even know what it is?"

"I don't know the exact genetic makeup. The lab delivers finished assets, and we show them to the public." She pressed an intercom button. "Can we drop a steer, please?"

Owen squinted out the window, still not seeing the *Indominus*. "How long has the animal been in here?"

"All its life."

"Never seen anything outside these walls?"

Claire raised one corner of her mouth. "We can't exactly take it for a walk."

Owen looked up at the cable system lowering the steer into the *Indominus*'s pen. "And you feed her with that?"

THUNK! The slab of raw beef dropped to the ground.

No animal emerged.

"Is there a problem with our methods?" Claire asked.

Owen cocked his head. "Animals raised in isolation, without parents, aren't always the most functional."

"Your raptors were born in captivity," Claire countered.

"With siblings. They learn social skills. And I imprint on them at birth. There's trust. The only positive relationship this animal has is with that crane," he said, pointing up. "At least she knows that means food."

Claire looked skeptical. "So she needs a friend? We should schedule playdates, that sort of thing?"

Owen ran his hand along claw marks in the glass. "Probably not a good idea."

Claire tapped her fingers on the glass anxiously. "Where is it? We were just here. *It* was just here."

In a back corner, the paddock supervisor looked up from a magazine. He checked the infrared monitors but didn't see the red outline of the *Indominus*. "Oh, boy . . . ," he muttered.

Claire turned to him. "What? What are you saying?"

"It doesn't make sense," the supervisor said. "The doors haven't been opened in weeks."

Owen looked at the inside of the paddock door through the window. "Were those claw marks always there?"

Claire looked. The door was scratched with long claw marks, as if something had climbed up the door. "You think it . . . ? Oh, god!"

She hurried toward the stairs, saying, "She has an implant in her neck. I can track it from the control room." She raced downstairs to her car, leaving Owen behind.

As she drove to the Control Center, Claire called on her cell phone. "We have an asset out of containment. Put Asset Containment Unit on alert. This is not a drill."

Chapter Eight

Flanked by the supervisor and a worker, Owen entered the paddock through a security entrance in the wall. He passed a jagged, broken tree stump. "She knock that down?"

"Yup," the supervisor said. He pointed at another stump. "That one, too."

Owen ran his fingers over the claw marks in the door.

"That door's thirty feet high," the supervisor said. "You really think she could have climbed out?"

"Depends," Owen said.

"On what?"

"On what kind of dinosaur they cooked up in that lab."

In the control room, the words "CONTAINMENT ALERT" flashed onto the biggest screen. "Wait, what?" Lowery asked, startled.

His phone rang. When he answered it, he heard Claire

yelling, "Lowery! Get me coordinates on the *Indominus*!"

Lowery started tapping his touchscreen. Masrani entered, straight from lunch, wiping his mouth. "What's happened?"

Lowery checked the *Indominus*'s coordinates, beamed from its electronic implant. "It's still in the cage."

"That's impossible," Claire said over the phone. "I was just there."

"I'm telling you, she's in the cage," Lowery insisted. He put a video feed from the *Indominus* paddock up on the screen. It showed Owen, the supervisor, and the worker. No *Indominus*. "Wait. There's people in there."

"Get them out!" Claire yelled. "Now!"

Vivian tapped her headset. "Paddock Eleven, this is Control. You need to evacuate the containment area."

In the paddock, Vivian's voice came over the supervisor's walkie-talkie. "Paddock Eleven, do you copy?"

Owen, studying the claw marks, looked back over his shoulder at the supervisor. His eyes widened, realizing what Vivian meant.

But the supervisor didn't. He spoke into his walkie-talkie. "What's the problem?"

"It's in the cage!" Vivian said. "It's in there with you!"

The three men started to run back toward the security entrance in the wall. *THWUUUMMP!* A massive white foot slammed down, blocking the way!

The supervisor and Owen ran toward the main door. But a clawed hand snatched the third man off the ground!

Owen looked up at the huge *Indominus rex,* gulping down the worker, boots sticking out of her jaws.

The supervisor opened the big door to escape.

Masrani, Lowery, and Vivian watched the control room screen in horror as the *Indominus rex* snapped its jaws in the air and ran toward the big open door.

"Close the door!" Masrani cried.

"You can't lock them in there with that thing!" Lowery protested.

"Close it now!" Claire yelled over her phone.

At the *Indominus*'s paddock, the massive steel door started to slide shut. Owen ran for it and slipped through.

CLANK! Before the doors could shut, the *Indominus* wedged itself into the gap. The machinery controlling the door strained to close it.

But with a huge push, the *Indominus* squeezed through the opening.

The beast was outside its cage. Free!

Owen slid under an excavator. He watched in silence as the *Indominus* looked around, sniffing the air.

The paddock supervisor crouched behind a pickup truck, praying the beast would leave him alone.

WHAM! The *Indominus* flipped the truck over like it was just a toy. "No . . . no!" the supervisor gasped.

The dinosaur grabbed the man with its long teeth, tossed him in the air, and chomped down on him. The air was filled with the sickening sound of snapping bones.

And she was still hungry. Now that she was free, she wanted to hunt. She sniffed the air, and then whipped her head around, staring right at Owen.

He quickly pulled out his knife, cut the excavator's fuel line, and poured gasoline all over himself.

The *Indominus* lowered her head until her nostrils were only two feet from Owen. She sniffed again . . . and quickly reared her head back at the smell of the gasoline.

The mighty beast turned and wandered away into the jungle. Owen exhaled, happy to be alive.

Claire entered the control room. Everyone stared at her, stunned. On their screens, they'd just seen two of their fellow employees devoured by the *Indominus rex*.

"Okay," Claire said. "Everyone remain calm. It can't get far. Its implant will shock it if it gets too close to a perimeter fence."

Lowery was staring at a screen. "It's moving. Fast."

Vivian spoke into her headset. "This is Control. Put out a park-wide alert for—"

"Hang up that phone," Masrani ordered.

Vivian looked at him, and then spoke again. "Uh, cancel that. Getting new information now. Everything's fine." She looked at Masrani for an explanation. Why didn't he want her to put out a park-wide alert? That beast was out there, running loose!

"Let Asset Containment capture it quietly," Masrani said. "The very existence of this park is predicated on our ability to handle incidents like this. It was an eventuality."

Lowery snorted. "You should put that in the brochure: 'Jurassic World: Eventually one of those things is gonna eat somebody.'"

Masrani glared at him.

"That paddock is four miles from the closest attraction," Claire said. "Asset Containment can handle this. No one else is going to get . . ." She hesitated.

"Eaten," Lowery said, finishing her sentence for her.

Chapter Nine

In the security barracks, an alarm blared as the Asset Containment Unit (ACU) prepared to go after the *Indominus*. Eight men in navy blue jumpsuits with ACU arm patches put on claw-proof vests and grabbed electric rifles.

Captain Hamada, a former SWAT team leader for the Tokyo police, twisted the handle on an electric spear. Blue sparks crackled from the tip.

Outside the *Velociraptor* research stables, Barry guided two handlers as they used long poles to fasten leather claw guards over Delta's talons. Delta didn't seem to like the claw guards, so Barry was trying to keep her calm.

"Easy, Delta," he said in his native French. "Easy now, girl."

Hoskins stood behind Barry, observing. "How fast can they run?"

"Fifty miles per hour. Sixty when they're hungry."

Delta flailed her clawed arm. Hoskins was startled, but the handlers had her under control. Barry's phone buzzed. He looked serious as he read the text.

"Code Nineteen up north. They say we lost two guys."

"What's a Code Nineteen?" Hoskins asked.

"Asset out of containment," Barry explained. "That new dinosaur—the big one." He shook his head. "These people, they never learn."

Hoskins eyed the raptors, thinking. "They're gonna learn all kinds of things about their asset now."

He walked away into the shadows, dialing his phone. "It's me. Looks like we may have an opportunity."

Gray and Zach were riding the monorail. They passed over Gallimimus Valley. Below them, tourists in a safari Jeep laughed as a herd of *Gallimimus* ran alongside them.

Gray was watching them through the monorail window, thinking that looked like fun. Then he spotted something. On the other side of the valley, an ACU transport vehicle raced toward an unknown destination.

Along a shaded river, *Apatosauruses* grazed, munching on the vegetation. Park guests on the Cretaceous Cruise paddled by in glass-enclosed kayaks.

VROOM! Behind the grazing dinosaurs, the ACU transport zoomed by, leaving a trail of dust. It was tracking the signal from the *Indominus*'s electronic implant. The men inside were determined to stop the *Indominus* before it got anywhere near these park visitors.

Inside the control room, Claire, Masrani, and the control team employees watched the video feeds from the ACU transport vehicle's cameras. "Such bravery in the face of danger," Masrani said. "I'd go with them if I could."

Lowery shot Masrani a doubtful look.

Just outside the room, a security guard called, "Sir? Sir! I need to see a badge!"

Owen burst in the room, ignoring the security guard. "What happened back there?" he demanded.

"You can't be in here—" Claire started to say.

"You have thermal cameras all over that paddock," Owen interrupted. "It couldn't just disappear."

"It must have been some kind of"—Claire searched for an explanation—"technical malfunction."

Owen couldn't believe what he was hearing. "*Technical malfunction!* Were you even watching? She marked up that wall as a distraction. She *wanted* us to think she'd escaped!"

Claire shook her head. "This is an *animal* we're talking about."

"An *intelligent* animal," Owen insisted.

"The ACU team is four hundred meters from the source of the beacon—the implant," Vivian said. She wanted to say, *"They've almost reached the monster,"* but that didn't sound professional.

Owen looked at the monitors and saw the ACU troopers carrying electric rifles and shock sticks. "You're going after it with *tasers?*"

"We have twenty-six million dollars invested in that asset," Masrani said. "We can't just kill it."

"They're right on top of it," Lowery said, studying a screen with satellite imagery.

Owen thought, *Those men are all going to die.* He'd seen what the *Indominus* could do. "Call them off," he said. *"Now!"*

"You are not in control here!" Claire snapped.

Owen watched the monitor, shaking his head, frowning. When it came to the hybrid dinosaur, it seemed no one was in control. . . .

Chapter Ten

The ACU transport vehicle rolled up to a shallow stream flowing through the jungle. The troopers got out, coordinating their movements. They were tense.

Moving in formation, they approached the stream. The guys in front held electric spears. The guys behind them had non-lethal electric rifles.

There was no sign of life anywhere.

Hamada spotted something lying on a rock. Something bloody. He nudged it with his foot.

It was the tracking device, no longer implanted in the *Indominus.*

The bloody implant appeared on the screen in the control room as Hamada held it up to his wrist camera. His voice came over the room's speakers. "Blood's not clotted yet. She's close."

Masrani squinted at the big screen. "What is that?"

"Her tracking implant," Owen said. "She clawed it out."

Claire looked confused. "How would it know to do that?"

Owen walked closer to the screen. "She remembered where they put it in."

Back at the riverbed, Hamada felt something warm on his hand.

A drop of blood.

It ran down one side of his hand. Another drop fell beside it, but this one ran down the other side of his hand. He noticed the other ACU troopers. They looked confused. Then they looked terrified.

Something huge was moving. Among the green leaves and vines of the jungle, it was becoming visible. Right next to them.

The *Indominus.*

"It can camouflage!" Hamada shouted into his headset as he backed away.

THWAM! The *Indominus* snatched Hamada off the ground, gripping him tightly in its long claws. "Open fire!" he yelled. "Take it down!"

The troopers fired electric cartridges. One lodged in the dinosaur's leg, sending a powerful shock pulsing through her body.

It only made her angrier.

The *Indominus* hurled Hamada to the ground, stomped on him, and swiped another trooper with her tail. The troopers fired nets at her, but she easily tore them off and chomped another trooper.

The remaining troopers picked up their fallen comrades and stumbled back toward the vehicle. One of them pulled out a real weapon and fired live ammo at the *Indominus*. The bullets pinged off the bony plates on her back as she turned and raced into the jungle.

Claire, Owen, and Masrani watched the heart monitors of the fallen troopers flatline. They stood stock-still, silent, appalled by what had happened.

"God, what have we done?" Masrani finally said in a low voice.

Owen looked up at the huge screen tracking every warm body in the park. There were thousands of them. "Evacuate the island."

"I can't," Claire said. "We'd never reopen."

Owen turned to her, staring in disbelief. "You made a genetic hybrid and raised it in captivity. She's seeing all this for the first time. She doesn't know what she is. She'll probably kill anything that moves."

Now it was Masrani's turn for disbelief. "You think the animal is contemplating its own existence?"

"She's learning where she fits into the food chain," Owen said. "I'm not sure you want her to figure it out." He stepped forward, staring at the map of the park with its thousands of visitors. "Asset Containment can use live ammo in an emergency. There's a minigun in the armory. Send up a chopper. Use infrared to find her."

Claire shook her head. "There are families here. I'm not going to turn this place into a war zone."

"You already have," Owen said.

"Mr. Grady," Claire said, trying to control her anger, "if you're not going to help, there's no reason for you to be in here."

Owen glared at Claire. "I don't need to be in here to help." He turned and stomped out, pausing next to Masrani along the way. "I'd have a word with the guys in your lab," he said in a low voice. "That *thing* out there. That's not a dinosaur."

Masrani took this in, deeply affected.

Claire watched Owen go. A small part of her wished he would stay. She turned back to the room, all eyes on her. "What's the live count?" This was the phrase they used for the number of guests currently in the park.

Lowery tapped his keyboard. "It's 20,857."

Claire looked at her boss. "I have to close everything north of the resort."

Masrani nodded. He didn't like it, but had no choice.

Claire addressed everyone in the control room. "Okay, people, this is a Phase One, real world. Bring everyone in."

They all turned to their headsets, phones, and keyboards, getting to work, sending out alerts, just as they'd practiced. Every person on the island who was north of the resort area had to be brought into the resort. Immediately.

Including Gray and Zach . . .

Chapter Eleven

The two brothers were standing in the VIP line waiting to get in a gyrosphere. The gyrospheres looked like giant hamster balls—plexiglass globes you could sit in, always staying upright while they spun through the countryside, passing close to the dinosaurs.

"What they didn't know at the time," Gray said, "is the soft tissue is preserved because the iron in the dinosaurs' blood generates free radicals."

Zach wasn't really listening to his little brother's lecture on the preservation of DNA. He was looking around at the other guests in line—people from all over the world.

"And those free radicals are highly reactive," Gray continued, oblivious of his brother's inattention, "so the protein and cell membranes get all twisted up and act as a natural preservative. DNA can survive for millennia that way."

Zach noticed the teenage girl he'd seen on the ferry. She was just ahead of them, climbing into a gyrosphere with her friend. She glanced at him and smiled. He smiled back.

"So now even if the amber mines dry up," Gray chattered on, "they'll still have bones to—"

"Shh," Zach hissed. "Shut up."

Gray turned to see what his brother was looking at. Girls. He should have known. "I thought things would be different without your dumb girlfriend around."

"Look, you don't get it, but you'll understand one day."

"No, explain it," Gray insisted. "What can you do with those girls that you can't do with me?"

The girls overheard that and giggled. Zach gritted his teeth. "Thanks, man."

"You're welcome," Gray said politely.

The ride operator motioned the two boys forward. "Okay, fellas. You ready?" Zach led Gray into the gyrosphere behind the one with the two girls just as their ball left the station. The operator shut the door. "Enjoy the ride," he said automatically.

The sphere lurched forward and rolled away from the platform on a track leading into the open grassland.

A phone rang. The ride operator held the next sphere back and answered it. "Hello." He seemed stunned by what he heard. "Seriously?"

He hung up and opened his employee handbook. He found the right page and started reading out loud. "Sorry, folks, ride's closed. Everyone"—he turned the page—"return to the monorail and proceed to a designated safety area."

The visitors in line were not at all happy with this announcement. One said in Spanish, "I waited in line with three kids for an hour!" Another yelled in Chinese, "Do you know how much we paid for this trip?"

The ride operator held both hands up. "Come on, guys. I just work here."

Inside their gyrosphere, Zach put his hand on the joystick, ready to drive. A screen lit up with an instructional video of a funny man dressed in a khaki safari outfit.

"Oh, hello," he said. "I was just doing a little predator tracking. Hobby of mine. I bet you're wondering how to drive this thing. Maybe I can help."

The video showed how the controls worked. "The gyroscopic technology means you'll always stay upright," the narrator explained.

In an animation, a gyrosphere got too close to a dinosaur. A red circle blinked around the sphere, and the dinosaur backed off. "And good news for bad drivers: our invisible barrier system will make sure you don't get into an accident."

"That sucks," Zach joked. "You can't even hit them."

"Where *are* they?" Gray asked impatiently.

Zach pushed the joystick. The gyrosphere lurched forward, rolling into a lush green valley where visitors could steer their globes close to roaming herbivores.

Gray and Zach rolled between a pair of *Apatosauruses*. Their gyrosphere came close to the huge dinosaurs' swooping heads. Gray laughed, loving it. Zach steered them around a *Triceratops* and right into the path of a lumbering *Stegosaurus*.

"Watch out!" Gray cried. "He'll get us!"

Zach stopped and reversed the sphere, allowing the *Stegosaurus* to pass. The two brothers were having a great time together.

Then an announcement came through the speakers inside the gyrosphere: "Due to technical difficulties, Jurassic World is now closed. Please disembark all rides and return to the resort."

"No!" Gray cried. "That was only point two miles!"

Zach watched the girls in the ball ahead of them turn back toward the station at the base of the valley. Then he looked at Gray and saw how disappointed he was. "Come on," Zach said. "We can stay out a couple more minutes."

Gray looked torn. He hated cutting the ride short, but he also didn't want to get in trouble. "But they said we have to go back."

"Aunt Claire gave us VIP passes," Zach said. "That means special privileges." He put a finger to his lips, turned the volume on the speakers all the way down, and pushed the joystick forward.

The gyrosphere rolled into a grove.

Chapter Twelve

Claire watched the monitors in the control room. She saw crowds gathering in the monorail stations, flooding onto the trains. One family held hands, moving together. Family—that reminded her . . .

She slipped into a side office and quickly dialed her cell phone. "Zara, listen. Take the boys back to the hotel right away."

She listened to her assistant, then froze. "Slow down. They what?"

As the boys' gyrosphere rolled through the grove, Zach's cell phone buzzed. "Hi, Aunt Claire."

Back in the office, Claire paced nervously. "Zach! Thank god! Is Gray with you?"

"We're out in the hamster ball thing," Zach said. "I can't hear you."

Claire spoke into her phone frantically. "Zach, listen

to me. You need to come back to the—"

But the call had dropped. Zach checked the reception bars on his phone. The screen said, "Service Unavailable." He didn't look at all upset. "That should be an app. It drops the call when you're getting yelled at."

Then he spotted something up ahead. "What happened here?"

He drove the gyrosphere up to a broken gate in the heavy wall enclosing the area. Bars twisted in all directions. Beyond the busted gate lay a small grove with grazing *Ankylosauruses*.

Zach's eyes lit up. "Dude. Off road."

Gray looked worried. "This isn't on the map. We're supposed to go back."

"I'm just concerned that you're not getting the full Jurassic World experience," Zach said, grinning.

He rolled the gyrosphere through the broken gate.

Freaking out, Claire returned to the control room, heading straight for Lowery. He was busy working his keyboard.

"Are there any gyrospheres left in the valley?" she asked urgently.

Lowery touched his screen, bringing up a new display. "They're all docked or headed back."

Claire was relieved. Then Lowery spotted something. "Wait, we have one in the field."

Claire's relief instantly evaporated. "It's going the opposite direction of where it should be going," Lowery added.

"Send some rangers out there to bring them in," Claire ordered.

Vivian spoke into her headset. "Security, we need a search and rescue team in the valley."

From the other end of the line came a blast of crowd noise. Then a ranger spoke above the crowd. "It's gonna be a while. We've got our hands full out here."

Claire grabbed Vivian's headset, pulling it to her mouth, which twisted Vivian's head around. "There are two guests missing!" she barked. "You need to make this your top priority."

"Ma'am," the ranger said, "we've got more than two guests missing. We'll do the best we can."

Claire tightened her mouth in frustration and let Vivian's head go. "Is there someone, anyone, who can come with me?" she asked, addressing the room.

"You mean someone here?" Lowery asked.

"We're kind of indoor people," Vivian said.

Exasperated, Claire looked at the monitors. She spotted Owen being manhandled by security guards outside the Genetics Lab. She made a decision and walked briskly out of the control room.

In the visitors' center, Claire hurried through the crowded chamber. An announcement came over the speakers: "Due to technical difficulties, all our exhibits are now closed."

As their parents rushed them along, kids tapped the display screens, making realistic holograms of dinosaurs pop up. A kid screamed as his sister surprised him with a hologram of a *Velociraptor*. Claire passed right through the holograms, paying them no attention.

Finally she spotted Owen near the front entrance. "Owen!"

He turned and looked at her questioningly as she ran up to him.

"I need you," Claire said.

"Finally you're being honest," Owen said.

"I need your *help*. My nephews are out in the valley. Please. If anything happens—"

Owen could see the fear in Claire's eyes. He took her aside. "How old are they?"

Claire thought a moment. "One of them is high school age. The other's a few years younger."

Owen looked surprised. "You don't know how old your own nephews are?"

"No, okay?" she snapped.

Zach and Gray rolled into a shady grove where the sun was blocked by a dense canopy of trees. The ground was rocky and uneven, covered by dead leaves.

"We're gonna get arrested!" Gray cried. "They'll shave our heads! And if we want root beer, we'll have to make it in the toilet!"

"What are you *talking* about?" Zach asked, completely bewildered.

They came upon four *Ankylosauruses* grazing in an area surrounded by rocks and tall trees. "See?" Zach said triumphantly. "There. You're welcome. Up close and personal with four dinosaurs."

"Ankylosaurus," Gray said. "We shouldn't be here. And there are five dinosaurs."

Zach screwed up his face and cocked his head. "Aren't

you supposed to be a genius? One, two, three, four!"

Gray pointed at a reflection in the gyrosphere's plexi-glass. "Five," he said.

Zach squinted at the reflection. The *Ankylosauruses* began to run away. Zach turned around and looked out the back of the gyrosphere. A huge dinosaur rose from the trees behind them. He didn't know its name, and for once, neither did Gray.

Chapter Thirteen

*I*ndominus rex sprinted forward to attack! Zach tried to steer clear, but the beast head-butted the gyrosphere into the *Ankylosaurus* stampede. The *Indominus* roared, rattling the sphere's plexiglass. The alpha *Ankylosaurus* turned to face the attacker, and the boys were caught right between the two combatants.

"Go! Go!" Gray cried.

"I'm trying!"

The gyrosphere moved, but the *Indominus* cut in front of it, blocking its path. Zach yanked the joystick left. "Not that way!" Gray screamed.

WHACK! The *Ankylosaurus* hit the gyrosphere with its mace-like tail, shattering a spiderweb crack in the plexiglass. The ball lifted off the ground, flew a few feet through the air, and cracked against a rock. The gyroscopic mechanism broke. From now on, when the ball rolled, the boys rolled, too.

When the ball finally stopped, the brothers were

hanging upside down inside it. They watched as the *Indominus* attacked the *Ankylosaurus* with its long, sharp claw. "We're safe in here, right?" Gray asked, terrified.

"Of course we are!" Zach said. "These things are dino-proof! They'd have to be, right?"

BRRZZZT! Zach's cell phone lay at the bottom of the sphere, buzzing.

It was Claire, calling as she climbed into a Jurassic World SUV with Owen behind the wheel. "Pick up, pick up, pick up," she pleaded.

Zach was trying. He reached his arm toward the phone.

"Zach . . . ," Gray whispered.

"Almost got it," Zach said, stretching his fingers.

Gray looked up and saw the *Indominus* staring at them from above. "Zach . . . Zach . . ."

TICK. TICK. The beast tapped on the glass with her claw. *CRACK!* The boys screamed as the claw broke through the glass! The *Indominus* brought her massive jaws down on the gyrosphere, trying to wrap its mouth around it. The boys stared down its throat. Its breath fogged the glass. Its teeth cracked the glass. Just when it seemed the ball was too big for the creature's mouth, it unhinged its jaw, widening its bite.

The brothers desperately kicked their feet. The *Indominus* lifted the sphere three feet off the ground and slammed it down onto the rocks! *CRASH!* The bottom of the sphere broke, leaving an open hole.

Zach saw a way out.

He unbuckled his belt, then helped Gray unbuckle his. "Get ready to run. You ready?"

The *Indominus*'s mouth was completely around the gyrosphere now, stopped only by the metal rings that held it together. Zach pulled Gray free, and they scrambled out the open hole and onto the rocks. The *Indominus* lifted the sphere—

"Run!" Zach cried. Then he grabbed Gray. "No, wait!"

Zach sheltered Gray with his body as the *Indominus* smashed the globe down around them again. It lifted the sphere once more.

"NOW! RUN!" Zach yelled.

The boys took off. The *Indominus* whipped the broken ball around, sending it flying. Her nostrils flared as she sniffed the air, turned, and followed the boys.

Zach and Gray ran through narrow woods. "Go, go, go!" Zach cried.

"I'm going!" Gray replied, just as the *Indominus* crashed

through the jungle behind them.

At the end of the long, sloping grove, the boys ran right up to the edge of a waterfall that dropped twenty feet into a pool. They stopped. Looked back.

The *Indominus* was charging straight toward them.

"Jump!" Zach shouted.

"I can't!" Gray said. The waterfall seemed way too high.

"We have to!" Zach insisted. "Now! One, two—"

Zach grabbed Gray's hand and they jumped. The *Indominus* snapped the empty space they'd stood in a second before.

SPLASH! Zach and Gray hit the water and plunged deep below its surface. The *Indominus* looked over the edge, snorted in frustration, and stomped off into the jungle.

Gasping for breath, the boys broke the surface. Zach dragged his brother onto the muddy shore. Their arms were around each other as they choked on water and tears.

"You jumped!" Zach managed to say. "That was awe-some!"

"It had seventy four teeth," Gray said.

Zach laughed. So did Gray. Then their laughter quickly turned to tears. They sobbed, thankful to be alive.

Chapter Fourteen

Back in the control room, Lowery watched footage from the *Indominus*'s paddock. "Check this out," he said to Vivian, who slid her chair over. "It can camo, right?" he said. "But watch this infrared footage."

The red-purple outline of the dinosaur blended into the foliage.

Vivian's brow furrowed. "The only way it could hide from a thermal camera is if it could change its heat signature. But no animal can do that."

"This one can," Lowery said.

From behind them, Masrani said, "Show it again," trying to keep the anger out of his voice.

In the Genetics Lab, Masrani confronted Dr. Wu. "What purpose could we have for a dinosaur that can camouflage?"

Dr. Wu poured tea. "Cuttlefish genes were added to

help it withstand an accelerated growth rate. Cuttlefish have chromatophores that allow the skin to change color."

"It hid from thermal technology," Masrani said angrily.

Dr. Wu looked surprised. Even pleased. "Really?"

"How is that possible?"

The geneticist thought a moment, then said, "Tree frogs can moderate their infrared output. We used strands of their DNA to adapt it to a tropical climate, but I never imagined—"

"Who authorized you to do this?" Masrani snapped.

"You did," Dr. Wu said. "Bigger, scarier. 'Cooler' was the word you used in your memo."

The doctor got up and walked through the lab, carrying his cup of tea. Masrani followed him, staying close. "What you're doing here, Dr. Wu, what you've done . . . they'll shut down this park, seize your work, everything you've built. You are to cease all activities here immediately!"

Dr. Wu remained cool. "Nothing in Jurassic World is natural. We've always had to fill gaps in the genome with DNA from other animals. You didn't ask for reality. You asked for more teeth."

"I never asked for a monster," Masrani said.

The geneticist shrugged. "*Monster* is a relative term. To a canary, a cat is a monster. We're just used to being the cat."

Claire and Owen drove through Gyrosphere Valley in his beat-up SUV. "What is that?" Claire asked, spotting something.

It was an *Apatosaurus,* lying on its side, still.

Owen drove all around the dinosaur. "Are we safe in here?" Claire asked nervously.

He got out of the SUV and cautiously approached the *Apatosaurus,* running his hands along gashes on her front legs. He saw a bite mark at the base of its neck.

"It didn't eat her," he said. "It's killing for sport."

The *Apatosaurus* made a low sound. It was still alive. "Oh, no," Owen said, hurrying to its head. He rubbed it soothingly. "I'm sorry, girl. I'm sorry."

Though she was frightened of the huge animal, Claire forced herself to get out of the SUV and go to Owen's side. The *Apatosaurus* made one last murmur. Her eyes went still.

"Oh, no," Claire said. "Is she . . . ?"

Owen nodded. He looked at the tree line, angry. They

heard a muffled roar in the distance.

Owen walked over a small hill and discovered six more dead *Apatosauruses*. His eyes filled with rage.

Back in the SUV, Owen and Claire drove into the shady grove of trees. "There!" Claire cried, pointing. Claire and Owen got out of the SUV to investigate. They weren't happy with what they found: the shattered remains of an empty gyrosphere.

Chapter Fifteen

Owen carried a powerful rifle with him, meant for taking down a *T. rex*. He examined the broken gyrosphere and found something jammed in the metal rings. He pried loose a massive dinosaur tooth. Claire's face went white.

She spotted Zach's cell phone. Tapping it on, she saw he'd missed seven calls from her. She slumped to the ground, moaning, "No . . . no . . ."

"They made it out," Owen told her.

She looked up at him. He was pointing to the mud. There were footprints—sneaker prints. Claire felt a wave of relief rush over her.

They followed the footprints to the edge of the waterfall, where they abruptly stopped. "Oh, god," Claire said. "They jumped."

"Brave kids," Owen said.

Claire started screaming for them. "Zach! Gray!" Owen clamped his hand over her mouth. She struggled loose and said, "Hey! I'm not one of your trained animals!"

"Listen," Owen whispered. "Those boys are still alive, but *we* won't be if you keep screaming like that!"

Claire nodded. That made sense. "You can pick up their scent and track them, can't you?" she said, speaking quietly.

"I was with the Navy, not the Navajos."

"So what, then?"

"You go back. I'll find them."

"*We'll* find them," she said.

Owen shook his head. "You'd last two minutes in that jungle. Less in those ridiculous shoes."

"If anything happens to those boys, I—"

They stared at each other. Claire looked determined. She clearly wasn't going to back down. Owen sighed. "Okay, but let's get one thing straight. I'm in charge here."

He shouldered his rifle and climbed down the steep rocks. Claire followed.

They never noticed that they'd been standing in an enormous *Indominus rex* footprint.

Deep in the jungle, Zach and Gray splashed across

rocks in a river. "We won't have to worry about water since it's a rain forest," Gray said. "And caterpillars are high in protein. They can keep us alive for weeks."

"Mm-hmm," Zach said, even though he was thinking, *No way am I eating caterpillars.*

"You know, this is what it would've been like," Gray said.

"What?"

"If dinosaurs never went extinct. People just walking around scared all the time."

"People wouldn't be here if dinosaurs never went extinct," Zach said.

They emerged onto a narrow dirt road. Gray noticed a fresh pair of tire tracks. He knelt down and studied the tracks, figuring out which way they led. "That way," he decided, pointing.

The brothers ran down the road, but soon the tracks veered off into the vegetation. Worried, Zach and Gray followed the path of broken tree limbs down a hill until they came to a Jurassic World maintenance vehicle that had crashed into a rock wall.

The boys cautiously approached the vehicle. Zach peered through the shattered windshield. No one was inside. The driver's seat was ripped, its white stuffing stained with blood. Zach backed away, realizing what had probably clawed the driver out of the vehicle.

"Who did it?" Gray asked. "The white one?"

Zach took his brother's arm. "We shouldn't stay here."

As he backed away, Zach stumbled. He looked down and realized it was a staircase leading up to a vine-covered building that was being slowly swallowed up by the earth.

Though the boys didn't know it, the building was the visitors' center built for the original Jurassic Park in 1993. Long abandoned, it had been reclaimed by the jungle.

The brothers pushed through the front door. As they walked in, something cracked under Zach's foot. He kicked aside a broken bone. A collapsed *T. rex* skeleton lay on the ground, covered by vines and vegetation.

"Aunt Claire will probably send people out looking for us," Zach said. "We can wait here."

"It'll find us here," Gray argued.

"No, it won't. Stop it." Zach picked up one of the *T. rex* bones and wrapped it in an old piece of canvas. He pointed to Gray's fanny pack. "You have matches in there?"

Gray dug through his fanny pack and pulled out a

book of matches. He handed them to Zach, who lit the makeshift torch. By its light, Zach noticed a door marked "Vehicle Garage."

"C'mon," he said, leading the way through the door.

They pushed through a tangle of vines hanging down through the collapsed roof. Sunshine lit up the decayed garage. It had an old Jurassic Park vehicle in it.

"A 1992 Jeep Wrangler Sahara, beige," Gray said.

Zach popped the hood and looked at the engine. "You remember all that stuff from when Dad fixed up Grandpa's Malibu?"

Gray nodded.

They went back outside to the crashed Jurassic World vehicle, salvaged the battery, the spark plugs, and a can of gasoline attached to the back. They worked fast, on edge, listening for the slightest rustle of leaves. Zach heard the roar of a dinosaur in the distance.

"You think it's out there?" he asked.

Gray looked horrified.

"I mean, I know for sure that thing is definitely not out there," Zach said. "Totally safe." He handed his brother the car battery. "Here. Take this. You're stronger than me."

Gray smiled. They lugged the car parts back into the garage and started working on the old Jeep.

Chapter Sixteen

In a small cove on Isla Nublar, a private military transport boat cut through the water, approaching the beach. Armored tactical vehicles rolled off the boat's ramp. Men in polo shirts and sunglasses unloaded black cases marked "InGen."

Hoskins walked with an InGen contractor. "Did Masrani give you the green light yet?" the contractor asked.

"He will," Hoskins said confidently.

High above the cove, Barry stood atop a cliff, watching the InGen contractors. He spoke into his two-way radio. "Owen, we have a situation here." He heard nothing but static. "Owen, where are you?"

At that moment, Owen was making his way through thick jungle, pushing branches aside.

"I think we're going in circles," Claire said. "Shouldn't we draw up some kind of a search grid?"

Owen ignored her.

Claire moved ahead, scanning the trees, trying to

figure out whether they'd been in this part of the jungle before. Behind her, Owen knelt down. He'd found something on the ground.

"You know, I underestimated you," Claire admitted. "Judged you. I've been treating you like some kind of Neanderthal, but there's obviously a lot more to you."

She turned around and saw that Owen was still kneeling, but now his hands were full of dinosaur manure. "What are you *doing?*"

He rubbed the manure all over his arms. "I know you're used to watching your assets behind glass, but we're on their turf now and even the smell of rosebuds and sunshine is going to attract a predator."

She stood there staring at him. She couldn't believe he was rubbing *dinosaur manure* all over himself!

"You're next," he said, motioning to her. "Come on."

Claire shook her head vigorously. "No, I'm not. I don't smell, okay?"

Owen pulled her down and rubbed manure onto her legs.

"Get your hands off me!" Claire hissed.

He kept right on applying the manure. "Consider for one second I might know a little more about something than you do," he said. "Now just hold still."

She brushed him away, plunged her hands into the pile of manure, and slathered it on herself. Owen watched, surprised. She paused. "Did I miss a spot?"

He pointed to her neck. She applied manure to her neck and her face.

"Whoa," Owen said.

"What?"

"I didn't mean . . . you didn't have to put it on your face."

She glared at him. He tossed her a bandanna. She marched defiantly into the jungle, wiping dinosaur manure off her face.

Owen allowed himself a tiny smile as he followed her. "I'm just saying you overdid it a little."

In the control room, Lowery studied the park map on a screen. "Look at that. She's headed straight for the resort."

"Why would she come here?" Masrani asked.

"She can sense thermal radiation," Vivian explained. "Our emergency measures just put every warm body in one place."

Hoskins entered, holding his badge up for the security guard to see. "Hoskins, InGen," he announced.

"I know who you are," Masrani said impatiently.

"Then you know why I'm here," Hoskins said, walking in like he owned the place. "My team has spent two years working on an application that could hunt and kill that creature."

Masrani narrowed his eyes, giving Hoskins a hard glare. "Your program was meant to test their intelligence."

Hoskins nodded. "And we discovered something in the process. They can follow orders. The solution to this crisis is right in your hands."

A muscle twitched in Masrani's jaw. "Let me be as clear as I can," he said slowly. "No *Velociraptors* are to be set loose on this island."

"You're out of your mind," Hoskins said. "You've got twenty thousand people trying to get off this island. There aren't enough boats. That thing is a killing machine, and it won't stop—"

"And further," Masrani said, walking to within a foot of Hoskins, "I intend to personally look into your project to determine its viability within the moral principles of this company."

Hoskins eyed Masrani with clenched teeth. "Okay, so what's your next move, boss?"

On the control center's helipad, ACU troopers bolted a heavy turret gun into the cabin of Jurassic One. The lead trooper gave a thumbs-up, and other troopers loaded into the helicopter.

Vivian hurried across the roof alongside Masrani, who wore a tan flight suit and carried a helmet under his arm. "Sir," she said, "I just can't seem to reach your flight instructor."

"Never mind," Masrani said. "He's probably caught up in the evacuation."

"And you're sure there's no one else who can fly a helicopter?"

Relishing the adventure, Masrani answered, "We don't need anyone else."

He strapped on his helmet and climbed into the cockpit. A gunner threaded bullets into the heavy gun.

Masrani took the controls and gave Vivian a confident thumbs-up as the helicopter rose into the air, wobbling a little.

Vivian watched, took a deep breath and then exhaled, clearly worried.

Chapter Seventeen

In the garage attached to the old Jurassic Park visitors' center, Zach finished connecting a cable to the battery. Gray sat in the driver's seat, peering over the wheel.

"Okay," Zach called. "Turn it over!"

Gray turned the key. The Jeep chugged, coughed . . . and started!

"Ha-ha!" Zach cried triumphantly. "It works!"

Zach gave his brother a manly hug and got behind the wheel.

"But you failed your driver's test," Gray said, sliding over into the passenger seat.

"Only the driving part," Zach said.

As they made their way through the jungle, Claire and Owen heard the Jeep's motor revving in the distance. "You hear that?" Owen said.

They ran toward the sound. When they reached the

old garage, the Jeep was gone, but they saw fresh oil on the concrete. Leaning his rifle against the wall, Owen picked up Zach's hoodie, left behind.

"This one of theirs?"

Claire nodded, thrilled to see the jacket. It meant her nephews were still alive.

"That road'll take them straight to the resort. We have to get back," Owen said, checking out the other Jurassic Park Jeep. "How did they get one of these running?"

THOMMMP! Dust crumbled from the ceiling. Owen grabbed Claire and pulled her behind the old Jeep.

THOMMMP! THOMMMP! Through the broken ceiling, they saw it.

The *Indominus.*

As they held their breath behind the Jeep, the beast pushed its head into the garage, sniffing. Owen wished his rifle weren't across the room, leaning against the wall. Disliking the smell of dinosaur manure, the *Indominus* slowly pulled its head out. Claire exhaled, relieved.

CRASH! The decaying ceiling collapsed onto the Jeep. Claire and Owen crawled through the door into the visitors' center, Owen grabbing his rifle as he went.

SMASH! The *Indominus* threw the old Jeep into the

wall behind them, barely missing them.

They ran through the lobby of the visitors' center. Behind them, they could hear the *Indominus* roaring as it wrecked the garage, searching for its prey.

Claire and Owen ran outside, tearing through a field of ferns. They jumped over a fallen tree and slid down an embankment. Then they lay still in the mud, listening, their eyes wide with fear. The thundering footsteps of the *Indominus* came closer and closer.

Silence.

Then . . . *WHACK!* The *Indominus* rammed into the fallen tree, sending it flying down the embankment straight toward Owen and Claire. They ducked as the tree crashed into a pair of trees and stuck there, missing their heads by inches.

The *Indominus* peered over the edge of the embankment, growling. *Don't come down here. Please don't come down here,* Claire thought desperately.

FRRRR! A helicopter buzzed overhead. The *Indominus* looked up, narrowed its eyes, and raced away.

Still shaking, Claire and Owen cautiously climbed the embankment and looked into the distance. The *Indominus* was barely visible, quickly disappearing into the jungle.

"Call ACU," Owen said. "Tell them to send everything they've got."

Lowery was watching the view from the helicopter's camera in the control room when his phone rang. He saw it was Claire. "Where have you been?" he barked.

"We found her," Claire whispered through the phone. "South of the Gyrosphere Valley, between the park and the aviary. Hurry—she's moving fast."

"Wait," Lowery said, "are you *following* the dinosaur?"

"Yes," Claire answered. "Get ACU out here. Real guns this time."

"ACU's airborne," Lowery said. "They've commandeered the helicopter. Jurassic One is armed and dangerous."

Inside the helicopter, Masrani concentrated on his flying. Behind him, two ACU troopers scanned the jungle with infrared binoculars.

Vivian's voice came over a speaker. "We have eyes on the target, south of the aviary. Proceed and engage."

Masrani's face lit up. He was enjoying the adventure. "Look alive, boys!"

Owen and Claire emerged from the dense jungle onto a rocky cliff overlooking the Pteranodon Aviary, a colossal domed cage of steel and polycarbonate glass. Jurassic One flew right over their heads, hunting the *Indominus.*

The gunner inside the helicopter spotted something close to the aviary. "Ten o'clock," he said, indicating its position. "By the birdcage." The *Indominus* was at the base of the aviary, near where it met the mountain it was built into.

The *Indominus* was staring through the glass.

Chapter Eighteen

Getting his turret gun ready to shoot, the gunner waved to Masrani. "Swing it around. A little lower."

Remembering his training, Masrani worked the controls, lowering the helicopter to give the gunner a clear shot.

"Nicely done," the gunner said. "Hold her steady."

Below them, the *Indominus* peered through the milky glass of the aviary at a *Pteranodon* and three *Dimorphodons* pecking at the skeleton of a tuna. Then she heard the chopper and craned her neck toward the sound.

She camouflaged against the jungle floor.

But the gunner had been warned about the *Indominus*'s ability to camouflage. He removed the thermal scope. Then he fired the turret gun, jerking back from the recoil.

BOOM! A tree trunk near the *Indominus* splintered in half. She roared at the chopper. Then she turned toward the base of the aviary to avoid the gunfire. To shelter herself, she ripped through the glass and metal, and crashed through the dome.

Meanwhile, in the control room, Lowery saw a red outline flash around the aviary on the master map of the park. A breach. He brought up a security camera feed from the aviary and zoomed in on the *Indominus.* "Oh, no. No, no, no, no!"

Hoskins watched over his shoulder. "Looks like the fox got into the henhouse."

In the aviary, the *Indominus* roared at four *Pteranodons* on the ground. They hopped backward, spreading their wings aggressively. The *Indominus* sniffed and backed off, uninterested. She looked up, seeing the chopper's shadow on the frosted glass roof.

The *Indominus* turned back toward the *Pteranodons* and roared again, herding them out the hole in the broken dome. They stumbled back through the opening and took flight.

In the helicopter, the gunner saw the flying reptiles screeching right toward them. "Bring it up! *Up!*"

Masrani pulled the helicopter up and away from the *Pteranodons.*

But not fast enough.

WHACK! A *Pteranodon* hit the helicopter's spinning

blade. And then another. The chopper jolted and spun. Jurassic One crashed through the roof of the aviary. Leaving a gaping hole in the ceiling, the helicopter plummeted to the ground and crumpled like tinfoil. Before it hit, the *Indominus* ducked out of the broken hole at the base of the dome.

On the cliff, Claire covered her mouth in horror as smoke billowed out of the aviary. "Simon . . . oh, god . . ."

The employees in the control room reacted to the disaster. No one could possibly have survived that crash. Her voice breaking, Vivian said, "We have a breach in the aviary."

Lowery zoomed in his remote camera on the aviary and saw *Pteranodons* and *Dimorphodons* flying out of the hole in the roof.

The massive flock of flying reptiles streamed out of the aviary through the smoke, disoriented and furious.

Owen and Claire watched the sky fill with reptiles. "Get under the trees!" Owen shouted. "Move!"

They scrambled for cover, diving under the jungle trees. They looked up as the reptiles flew overhead, their shadows flicking on the ground. "They're heading toward the resort," Owen said.

In their Jurassic Park Jeep, Zach and Gray smashed through an old rusted gate and screeched onto a main access road. "We made it!" Zach said. "We're safe now!"

But Gray looked up and saw eight massive *Pteranodons* flying above them. His mouth dropped open.

Two Jurassic World rangers stood guard at a security gate in the fortified wall protecting the resort from the rest of the island. One of them spotted the old Jurassic Park Jeep zoom up the road toward them. "That's a first," he said, never having seen one of the old Jeeps moving.

Zach and Gray screeched to a stop in front of the wall. "Open it!" they screamed, pointing to the sky. "Open the gate!"

The rangers looked up. They saw a triangular formation of dozens of flying reptiles.

Claire and Owen emerged from the jungle and ran toward the aviary's employee parking lot. Her phone rang. "Hello?"

It was Zara. She was racing down the stairs of the visitors' center. "Claire! We spotted the boys on a surveillance camera feed! They're approaching the West Gate!

I'm headed there now!"

"Don't let them out of your sight," Claire said, relieved. "I'm on my way."

Owen jumped onto a Jurassic World all-terrain vehicle. "Get on."

Claire climbed on the ATV behind him. They sped off toward the resort.

Chapter Nineteen

Main Street was packed with angry, frustrated guests trying to entertain their children until the rides reopened. A new announcement came over the loudspeakers: "Ladies and gentlemen, due to a containment anomaly, all guests must take shelter immediately."

A father tried to reassure his three kids. "Anomaly? What kind of dinosaur is that? Sounds exciting, huh?"

But then he looked up. The sky was full of *Pteranodons* and *Dimorphodons*. And they were flying straight toward the resort. Fast.

The winged reptiles circled over the resort like vultures, eyeing the panicking tourists below. The lead *Pteranodon* dove toward Main Street. The others followed.

Tourists ran for cover as the reptiles knocked over food carts and shade umbrellas with their long, leathery wings. In the petting zoo, a *Pteranodon* tried to carry off a baby *Triceratops,* but it proved too heavy.

Alarms blared and warnings flashed throughout the control room. The screens showed fleeing tourists and destructive flying reptiles. Lowery and Vivian watched the disaster in horror. Behind them, Hoskins stared at the monitors, his eyes wide. Suddenly he rushed out of the room.

Up on the building's roof, Hoskins ran onto the empty helipad for a direct view of the chaos down in the resort. He looked strangely thrilled as he watched the terrifying action below.

Zach and Gray ran with Zara out of an alley onto Main Street. They saw the *Pteranodons* and *Dimorphodons* swooping down and attacking helpless tourists. "Oh, god," Zara gasped. "What's happening? What—"

WHOMP! A *Pteranodon* swiped Zara off the ground and carried her into the air, screaming. *WHOMP!* A second *Pteranodon* stole Zara from the first, snatching her right out of the other's claws. The two fought over their prey, flying out over the lagoon.

Then they dropped her.

Zara plummeted into the water. *SPLASH!* A hulking shadow moved in the lagoon. *THMMM! THMMM!* The two *Pteranodons* dove in after Zara, slicing through the water. One of them grabbed her in its jaws and swam to the surface.

With Zara in its mouth, the *Pteranodon* splashed about, flapping its wings, trying to take off. But the reptile couldn't get out of the water. Then *WHOOSH!* The *Mosasaurus* exploded out of the lagoon, engulfing the *Pteranodon* and Zara in one gigantic bite.

Owen and Claire ran onto the resort's boardwalk with ACU workers. Owen carried a rifle. The ACU workers battled the flying reptiles with electric spears and tranquilizer guns. Unfortunately, the tranquilizer guns brought huge *Pteranodons* and *Dimorphodons* crashing down onto the guests below.

Zach and Gray ran out onto the other end of the boardwalk searching for their aunt. Zach spotted a *Pteranodon* diving down at them. "Run!" he yelled.

They ran, but the reptile dove too fast. Zach grabbed his brother and shoved him out of the way as the *Pteranodon* skidded to a stop on the asphalt.

BRAAAAAK! A diving *Dimorphodon* attacked Owen. He struggled with the reptile, its wings flapping and its mouth screaming at him. Claire picked up a tranquilizer rifle and swung it like a bat, cracking the *Dimorphodon* in the face. She jabbed the rifle into the creature's belly and fired. It screeched and flew backward, sedated. Owen, amazed by Claire's actions, jumped up and kissed her.

Then Claire spotted her nephews through the crowd of panicking tourists. "Zach! Gray!"

"Aunt Claire?" Gray shouted.

Zach's eyes swept right past her, not recognizing this barefoot woman covered in blood and dirt and dinosaur manure.

Gray grabbed his arm and pointed. "That's her!" Then he looked again, unsure. "Is that her?"

They ran toward their aunt as she ran toward them. When they reached her, they expected to be yelled at, but Claire pulled them into a tight hug. She ran her hands over their faces and through their hair, finding blood on Gray's forehead.

"What is this? What happened to you? Where did you go? Why didn't you come back? Where's Zara?"

Owen trotted up behind Claire, dirty, carrying a rifle. The boys looked up at him. "Who's that?" Zach asked.

Claire stood up and straightened her hair. "We work together."

A team of InGen security contractors in polo shirts burst into the control room. Hoskins stormed past the security guard.

"Simon Masrani's death is a tragedy," he said. "The mission now is to prevent further loss of life."

Lowery and Vivian looked at each other, confused. "Uh, who are these guys?" Lowery said.

"Glad you asked," Hoskins answered. But he gave no further explanation.

Lowery looked alarmed as InGen contractors took over every position in the room.

"You're all relieved of duty," Hoskins told the Jurassic World employees. "I'm putting a new team on the ground."

Chapter Twenty

At sunset, a private military helicopter flew over the ocean toward Isla Nublar. InGen soldiers rode inside, carrying automatic weapons.

BRAAAAK! A stray *Dimorphodon* flew by in the opposite direction, shrieking at the chopper.

One of the soldiers lifted his weapon and shot a burst of gunfire at the flying reptile. It crumpled in midair and plunged into the sea.

The helicopter landed on the helipad. Hoskins ran under the whirling rotor blades and climbed in. Inside, an InGen contractor reported, "We're gearing up the animals now."

"How long till they're ready?" Hoskins shouted over the noise of the chopper.

"Hard to say," the contractor answered. "Some of the handlers are pushing back."

Hoskins smiled coldly. "Then push back harder."

The door slammed shut, and the helicopter rose into the sky.

Owen led Claire and the two boys through the crowds. Park employees scrambled to contain the chaos as best they could.

Claire pulled out her phone. "Lowery, I'm on my way back to you."

In the control room, Lowery checked over his shoulder and ducked into a side office. He spoke in a low voice. "Bad idea. Apparently the Jurassic World board assigned emergency powers to InGen's private security division. They've taken over in here. That guy Hoskins is in charge. He's got some insane plan to use the raptors."

Claire narrowed her eyes, angry at having her authority undercut by Hoskins. "What do you mean, 'use the raptors'?"

VROOM! The InGen helicopter buzzed overhead. It cut a straight path over the resort, flying past the chaos without stopping to help the people below. It was headed for the Raptor Research Arena on the east coast of the island.

Owen stared up at it, filling with rage. "Take the kids,"

he said to Claire. "Get off the island."

Before Claire could answer, they heard the screams of hundreds of frightened people. At the end of the alley, a wooden gate leading to Main Street burst open. Scared tourists stampeded down the narrow corridor straight at Owen, Claire, Zach, and Gray. They backed away from the mob, but there was nowhere to run.

Owen spotted a mobile veterinary unit behind them. "Get in!"

Zach and Gray scrambled into the fortified vehicle between Claire and Owen in the front seat. Owen gunned the engine, threw the vehicle in reverse, and backed away from the approaching tide of people. "Drive! Go!" Zach and Gray yelled.

BRRAAAAK! A *Pteranodon* landed behind the crowd and reared up, spreading its wings. If the tourists were panicking before, now they were going absolutely berserk, climbing over each other to escape from the creature.

Owen swerved into a side alley and backed away from the insanity. There was nothing he could do.

"Can we stay with you?" Gray asked.

"Oh, honey," Claire reassured him, "I will never leave you again, ev—"

"No, him," Gray and Zach said in unison.

She realized they meant Owen.

Night had fallen. Bright lights lit up the Raptor Research Arena. InGen workers unpacked military gear: infrared cameras, satellite tracking collars, and weapons.

The four *Velociraptors* were penned in steel squeeze cages. Bars hugged their bodies to keep them from attacking their handlers. They stared through the gates at the front of the cages.

Barry watched uneasily as a pair of contractors attached cameras with infrared lights to the raptors' heads. One of the contractors turned on a wireless tablet computer. On the screen, he watched the feed from the camera. He could see whatever the dinosaur was seeing.

Hoskins approached Delta, holding up his hand. "Hey, you!" he called. "Look up here! Right here!"

"It's a she," Barry said. "And she looks at what she wants. Usually what she wants to eat."

Delta looked straight at Hoskins, locking her eyes on his. On the tablet computer, Hoskins's face filled the small screen.

Headlights hit Barry, Hoskins, and the *Velociraptors*. It

was Owen, pulling up in the mobile veterinary unit. He jumped out of the vehicle and headed straight for Hoskins.

"Finally, the mother hen shows up," Hoskins sneered.

WHAM! Owen punched Hoskins, hitting him hard. Hoskins stumbled back into the dirt. Two of his InGen soldiers reached for their guns.

"No, no," Hoskins said, stopping them. They holstered their weapons. Hoskins wiped blood from his mouth and smiled. "Subtle," he said.

"Get out of here and stay away from my animals," Owen ordered.

Claire and the boys came up behind him. The four of them were covered in earth and sweat, scratched a little. They looked as though they'd been through a muddy, difficult obstacle course. And in a way they had—with dinosaurs as the obstacles.

"This isn't your territory anymore," Hoskins growled. "Don't forget—you work for me."

"You *wanted* this to happen!" Claire said accusingly.

Hoskins shook his head. "How many more people have to die for this mission to start making sense?"

"It's not a mission," Barry said. "It's a field test."

Hoskins paused a moment. Then he said, "This is an

InGen situation. We'll have cruise ships here at first light. Everyone on the island will make it out safe. And if you watch the news tomorrow, you'll see a story about how we saved lives. Or to be more accurate, *they* saved lives." He nodded toward the *Velociraptors*.

He stared at Claire and Owen. They had no argument for him. They had to do whatever they could to save the people on the island from the *Indominus rex*.

"This is happening," Hoskins said. "With or without you."

Owen looked at Barry. He didn't have to say what he was thinking out loud. *Could this plan of Hoskins's possibly work?*

Barry shook his head. "They've never been out of containment. It's crazy."

Owen looked at Claire. She slowly shook her head no.

But Owen knew he had no choice. Hoskins was clearly determined to use the raptors, no matter what. "If we do it, we'll do it *my* way," he said.

Chapter Twenty-One

O wen leaned over a map of the island, giving instructions to the InGen soldiers. "Okay, this is a scent drill. We've done it millions of times, only this time the pig's a little bigger. When they find it—and they will find it—they'll herd it into the kill zone. There's only one good target. Do *not* shoot my animals."

The soldiers, heavily armed, nodded and headed out.

"This could work," Barry said.

"That's what I'm afraid of," Owen said.

Owen went to check on the *Velociraptors*. He approached Blue carefully. She was bucking against her camera harness. "Easy," Owen said quietly. "Easy, Blue."

Blue drew close to Owen and tilted her head down. Owen reached through the bars of her cage and placed his hand on her snout. She lightly bumped Owen with it. He examined the camera strapped tightly to her forehead.

Zach and Gray came up behind Owen, looking cautiously at the *Velociraptors*. "Are they safe?" Gray asked.

"Not really," Owen answered honestly.

"What are their names?" Zach asked.

Owen pointed at the raptors one at a time. "That's Charlie. Delta. Echo. Out front is Blue. She's the beta." That meant she was second-in-charge.

"Who's the alpha?" Gray asked.

"You're talking to him, kid," Owen said.

Gray smiled. He thought Owen was awesome.

Claire walked up, eyeing the *Velociraptors* warily. "So this is who you've been spending all your time with?"

"What can I say?" Owen answered. "She gets me."

Claire managed to smile, even though she was worried about what might happen to Owen once he went out hunting the *Indominus rex* with these four dinosaurs.

Hoskins's voice came over a walkie-talkie. "What's the holdup? Let's roll."

Owen looked past Claire at the soldiers heading out. "This is a bad idea whether it works or not."

Zach and Gray got in the back of the mobile veterinary unit. Claire looked in through the back doors. "I'll be right up front," she said reassuringly. "If you need me, just open that window."

Gray saw the small window between the back compartment of the vehicle and the front.

"Put your seat belts on," Claire said. The boys looked

around the compartment. No seat belts. "Okay," she said. "Then just . . . hold hands."

She closed the door and locked it. The boys sat in the dark, lit only by a shaft of light through the small window. Gray clicked on a flashlight. His legs were trembling. "Nothing's coming in here, right?"

Zach realized his little brother was scared. "Remember the ghost in the garage at the old house?" he asked. "I protected you, right?"

Gray smiled, his face lit by the flashlight. "You made a battle-ax out of a ruler and a paper plate."

"See? Nothing can get you while I'm around."

"But you're not always going to be there."

Zach leaned his head against his brother's. "Yeah, I will. Hey, we'll always be brothers. And we'll always come back to each other, no matter what."

Zach put his hand on Gray's knee. It stopped shaking. "No matter what," Zach repeated.

Back by the *Velociraptor* pen, Owen unfolded a towel. Inside it was the bloodstained tracking device the *Indominus* had ripped from its own flesh. He walked down the line of cages, offering the scent to the raptors. They bucked and screeched, eager to find the source of that blood and kill it.

"Don't embarrass me," Owen told them.

In the control room, Lowery and Hoskins watched Owen give the scent to the raptors. "Incredible," Hoskins said.

Owen fastened a night camera to the handlebar of his vintage motorcycle and revved the engine.

Barry kick-started a Jurassic World ATV. He had a raptor shock stick strapped to his back, a tablet computer with a tracking system mounted to his handlebars, and a headset microphone. "Testing, testing."

Owen gave Barry a thumbs-up and looked over his shoulder at Claire in the mobile vet unit. He could see Zach and Gray peering through the small window behind her.

He held his hand up to signal the young handler whose life he'd saved earlier that day. The handler gripped the lever that would open the raptors' gates. Owen lowered his hand, and the handler pulled the lever, raising the gates.

The *Velociraptors* raced out into the night, searching for their prey.

Owen peeled out on his motorcycle, following the raptors. Behind him came Barry on his ATV, the InGen soldiers in tactical vehicles, and Claire and the boys in the mobile veterinary unit.

The night hunt for the *Indominus* had begun.

Chapter Twenty-Two

On his motorcycle, Owen sped up, joining the four running *Velociraptors*, a team of five on the hunt.

They reached a clearing in the dense rain forest. The raptors slowed down, lowering their heads to the ground.

Owen braked and shut off his motorcycle. "They found something," he told Barry in his headset.

The soldiers spilled out of their vehicles and took up positions among the moonlit trees on the edge of the clearing. A few of them climbed into the trees' lower branches. They aimed their weapons, waiting.

Everyone tensed. They could hear the *Indominus* approaching. The *Velociraptors* reared up and backed away as the jungle moved and the *Indominus* revealed itself, coming out of camouflage.

Hissing, the raptors surrounded their prey. The *Indominus* looked down at the circling raptors, cocking her head, considering them. Then she roared—a roar that sounded similar to the *Velociraptors'* own high-pitched screeches.

They tilted their heads at the sound, confused. They screeched back. And they relaxed their bodies, looking less aggressive.

"Something's wrong," Owen said.

"What do you mean?" Barry asked through their headsets. "What's wrong?"

The raptors circled the *Indominus,* curious, almost like a group of dogs checking out a new dog.

"They're communicating," Owen said.

He watched with dismay as Blue, Charlie, Delta, and Echo took their places at the side of the *Indominus.* The look in their eyes had changed. They were no longer hunting *Indominus.* The raptors were hunting humans.

Owen said, "I know why no one in this park would say what that hybrid is made of."

"Why?" Barry asked.

The *Indominus* and the *Velociraptors* roared together.

"That thing's part raptor," Owen said.

BLAM! The soldiers opened fire, hitting the *Indominus* with multiple rounds. Some bullets seemed to connect, but many deflected off its bony plates. Roaring, the *Indominus* smashed back into the jungle. A rocket-propelled grenade streaked across the clearing and hit a tree, exploding its branches into flames. The four raptors sped into the jungle, disappearing from sight.

"Watch your back!" Owen said. "The raptors have a new alpha!"

The battle was on. They all took off after the dinosaurs.

A soldier crept through the jungle. Hearing a twig crack behind him, he spun around and found himself face to face with Echo. But she didn't attack. Instead, the *Indominus* stepped into the moonlight behind the soldier. He whirled around and raised his rifle, but the *Indominus* swept it away, then raked her claws across the soldier's chest. He fell to the ground.

Nearby, two other soldiers spotted the *Indominus*. They opened fire but were immediately attacked by two raptors coming at them from both sides. It was over quickly.

Owen raced past the fallen soldiers near death. He spotted Delta crouched over a body in the distance, eating voraciously. A soldier fired a rocket propelled grenade right at Delta. *BOOM!* Owen was thrown back by the explosion. He rose to his feet, disoriented and devastated. Delta was gone.

In a nearby part of the jungle, Barry raced through the trees, pursued by a raptor. He slid into a hollow fallen tree. *THUNK.* The raptor landed on the tree. *CLICK. CLICK.* Her talons stuck in the wood as she walked the length of the hollow tree, coming closer to Barry.

Reluctantly, he drew his pistol and pointed it straight up through a hole in the wood, not wanting to fire. He pulled back the hammer. *CLICK.* He saw the raptor's eye through the hole. It was Blue. She screeched and clawed at the log, splintering the wood.

Owen's motorcycle roared in the near distance. Blue whipped her head toward the motorcycle's headlight. She narrowed her eyes and raced off after it.

Barry exhaled. Still alive. For now . . .

Chapter Twenty-Three

From the control room, Lowery watched the raptors' video feeds in horror. One of them was clearly devouring a soldier. "This what you guys had in mind?" he asked in a hoarse voice.

Hoskins didn't answer. Lowery looked over his shoulder. Hoskins was gone, and the InGen contractors were clearing out, packing up their equipment.

"What's going on?" Lowery asked.

"They said we have to evacuate," Vivian answered. "There's a boat."

Lowery looked up at the screens, feeling a strong sense of responsibility for one of the first times in his life.

In the Genetics Lab, workers hurried to put their creations in emergency storage. Dr. Wu stood by an incubator full of unhatched eggs, watching as a robotic arm moved each egg into a temperature-controlled case. Behind him, lab workers archived frozen embryos.

"Everything must be accounted for," he ordered. "I want all backup generators online."

He walked to a door in the rear of the lab and scanned his palm on a lock. The door slid open, revealing a secret room, glowing blue. He went in and closed the door. His phone buzzed.

"Where have you been?" Wu said into his phone.

In a side office near the control room, Hoskins spoke into his phone. "Change of plans. Mission took a jog to the left. I need all the new assets off-site."

Dr. Wu frowned. "The embryos are safe here. They can live up to eight weeks with the generators."

Hoskins growled, "This park will be shut down by morning. Our little side project is about to get a shot in the arm. I don't want a bunch of bankruptcy lawyers messing with something they don't understand."

Dr. Wu looked around him at the contents of the secret room. He felt trapped by the situation.

"I'll take that as a 'yes, sir,'" Hoskins said, hanging up.

Bursts of gunfire lit up the jungle. In the mobile

veterinary unit, Zach leapt up and opened the window to the front seat.

"Is everybody dead?" Gray asked, terrified.

"No, everyone's fine," Claire said.

"Don't lie to him," Zach said.

"He's scared," Claire said. "It's okay to lie when people are scared."

Gray moved closer to the window. "I'm ready to go home now."

"You will," Claire told him. "Tomorrow you'll be home. And your mother will never let you see me again. But we had this, right?"

THUNK. A soldier hit the windshield with his bleeding hand. "Run," he gasped.

Claire fumbled for the keys. The wounded soldier limped around to the back of the vehicle and opened the rear door. But the boys saw something behind him in the dark. Something terrifying.

"Close the door! Close it!" Zach shouted.

BOO A A 1RRR'\" hatho leapt out of the dark and dug her claws into the soldier's back.

"Drive!" Zach yelled. "Go!"

Claire revved the engine and started to shift into gear,

but—*SMASH!* Echo shattered the driver's-side window with her talons and ripped the seat with her teeth as Claire whipped her head out of the way just in time. Claire floored the gas. Echo fell away. The boys watched through the open back doors as Echo rolled in the dust, stopping beside Charlie. The boys exhaled as the vehicle left the raptors behind.

But then the *Velociraptors* saw the red taillights speeding away from them. They got up and raced after the mobile veterinary unit.

Though Claire was driving as fast as she could through the rough terrain, the raptors soon caught up. The boys screamed as they saw the fierce dinosaurs through the swinging back doors. Claire swerved hard and managed to knock Echo away.

But Charlie was still coming, trying to jump through the doors in the back. Zach grabbed an electric spear. As the boys struggled to turn it on, Charlie leaped into the moving vehicle, piercing the metal with her claws.

"Turn it on!" Zach yelled.

"I don't know how!" Gray screamed.

Hissing, Charlie reached for the boys. Zach found the blue button and pressed it. The tip crackled. The boys jabbed it into the raptor's chest. *TTZZZZHH!* Charlie screeched at the shock and tumbled out the back, taking the spear with her.

"Did you see what we did?" Zach yelled triumphantly.

"I can't wait to tell Mom!" Gray shouted.

"No!" Claire called back through the window. "You cannot tell your mom about that! Ever!"

VROOM! Owen sped up alongside Claire's window. "We have to get indoors! Follow me!"

He raced ahead. Claire took off after him.

Charlie, still weak from the electric shock, got to her feet. Echo appeared from the dark, disoriented and angry. Blue emerged from the jungle and stepped to the front of the pack. She looked down the road at the distant taillights.

Blue raised her head and screeched. Charlie and Echo joined in.

Elsewhere in the jungle, the *Indominus* raised her head, listening. She roared in response and raced toward the three *Velociraptors.*

Chapter Twenty-Four

Lowery was alone in the control room when the phone rang. "Lowery, we're coming to you," Claire said. "Call in a helicopter."

"I already did," he said. "Just get here now."

Claire and Owen drove to the visitors' center, passing through the abandoned Main Street. They parked the vehicles and jumped out. With the two boys, they ran for the control room. But when they passed the Genetics Lab, they noticed shadows moving inside. "That's odd," Claire said. "They evacuated the lab."

They entered the hidden laboratory, lit only by glowing walls of technology. They saw small cages and tanks holding experimental genetically modified creatures. A strangely muscular mouse. A monkey with bat wings. A fish with tiny clawed hands and feet.

"What is all this?" Claire said.

In the doorway behind them, Hoskins said, "I'm afraid that's above your pay grade, hon."

The four of them spun around to face Hoskins.

"Where's Henry?" Claire asked.

"Dr. Wu works for us," Hoskins said. He motioned to InGen contractors, who rolled away a cold-storage unit on wheels. It was stacked with blood samples and embryos.

Looking at a monitor, Gray said, "That's not a real dinosaur." The screen showed a rotating 3-D model of a hybrid "Stegoceratops"—a mixture of *Stegosaurus* and *Triceratops*.

"No, it ain't, kid," Hoskins agreed.

The image on the screen changed. It showed a 3-D model of the *Indominus rex*.

Hoskins said, "Imagine that one, a fraction of its size, intelligent, deadly, able to hide from our most advanced military technology."

SMASH! A rack of glass vials shattered in the main lab. Owen and Claire pressed the boys back against the wall. Hoskins froze, able to see something in the room that the others couldn't see.

TICK. TICK. Claws tapped on the floor, approaching the door.

Echo peered around the corner, hissing.

Owen, Claire, and the boys hid in the shadows. The *Velociraptor* backed Hoskins up against a wall. "Easy, now," he said. "Easy, boy."

Echo hissed again. Without turning his gaze from the raptor, Hoskins called out, "Owen, what do I do? Owen!"

Owen covered Claire and the boys with his arm, keeping them still.

Hoskins stood up straight and held out his hand, trying to copy the gesture he'd seen Owen use to control the raptors. "There you go, boy. See? I'm on your side."

Echo cocked her head, seeming to relax. She took another step closer.

"That's right," Hoskins said. "I'm on your side."

RRRAAWWMMMP! Echo bit Hoskins's hand off in one ferocious bite. Hoskins screamed, and Echo attacked.

Owen, Claire, and the boys ducked behind a steel counter. When Echo's tail knocked over a tower of animal cages, Owen saw an opportunity. The cages lay between Echo and the door. Owen grabbed Claire's hand, and all four of them ran back into the main lab.

They passed through the lab and into the hallway. Claire pointed toward the elevator bank. "This way!"

SMASH! Charlie threw herself through the glass ahead of them. Shards of glass crunched beneath the raptors' feet as Owen, Claire, Zach, and Gray spun around and ran back toward the visitors' center.

Echo joined Charlie in the chase.

Chapter Twenty-Five

On the roof, InGen contractors finished loading the cold-storage containers into a helicopter's cargo bay. They climbed into the chopper, where Dr. Wu was waiting anxiously. "Where's Hoskins?" he asked.

"He didn't make it," one of the contractors answered.

Dr. Wu took in the news of Hoskins's death. "But he left provisions? Our deal is still intact?"

"Don't worry," the contractor said. "You'll be well taken care of."

The chopper rose into the night sky above Isla Nublar.

In the visitors' center, Owen, Claire, Zach, and Gray sprinted through the neo-paleontology display, trying to reach the front door. As he passed displays, Zach swiped his hands across screens, bringing up dinosaur holograms.

A trio of realistic *Dilophosauruses* appeared, roaring and spitting. The pursuing *Velociraptors* slid to a stop and took up attack positions. The holograms bought the four humans just enough time to escape through the front door.

They ran onto Main Street. *ROAR!* Blue lunged out of the dark, baring her teeth. Hissing, Echo emerged through a broken window in the visitors' center—the same window the raptors had used to enter the building. Charlie followed close behind.

The three *Velociraptors* surrounded Owen, hissing aggressively. He and Claire held the boys close. Blue moved close to Owen, examining him as if she were deciding how to kill her prey. Their faces nearly touched.

"That's how it is, huh?" Owen said.

Blue hissed. But she didn't attack. Something deep inside her seemed to recognize Owen. He slowly raised his hand, letting Blue see it. "When she was born," he said quietly, "she looked up at me, right into my eyes, like this."

He raised his open hand higher. Blue recoiled. "Easy . . . easy . . ."

Owen reached out and removed her camera harness. She allowed it. There was a quiet moment between them.

THOOM! THOOM! The *Indominus* was coming.

"Owen . . . ," Claire said.

The *Indominus* roared in the distance, getting closer.

Blue backed away. "No, no," Owen said. "Stay with me. Come on, girl."

Claire, Zach, and Gray looked at each other. *What was happening?*

THOOM. THOOM. The white-gray *Indominus rex* emerged from the dark, stomping down the middle of Main Street in the moonlight. Blue looked over her shoulder at her new alpha, then back at Owen.

The *Indominus* reached them. She roared behind Blue. She wanted Blue to attack.

But Blue whipped her head around and snapped protectively.

Anger surged through the *Indominus.* She reared up and swiped her long claw, throwing Blue aside. The *Velociraptor* slid across the ground, writhing and howling, deeply injured.

Charlie and Echo watched. They looked back at Owen, then up at the *Indominus.*

Which alpha would they choose?

Echo and Charlie moved back to Owen's side. The raptors faced the *Indominus* in attack positions. Owen allowed himself a tiny smile, knowing he had them back. He slowly motioned toward a shiny steel merchandise booth stacked with hats, stuffed animals, and *T. rex* soda cups. "Get the boys inside."

Claire slowly took Gray's hand. Gray took Zach's hand. "Ready?" Claire said. "And . . . now."

They ran for the booth. The *Indominus* followed their movement, but Owen gave a sharp whistle—an attack signal to his raptors!

Charlie and Echo leapt onto the *Indominus*'s back, digging their teeth in. Owen ducked her swinging tail. Both raptors sunk their claws into the beast's back.

Zach, Gray, and Claire vaulted over the counter into the booth.

Charlie screamed as the *Indominus* grabbed the raptor with her long, sharp teeth and flung her to the ground. Echo dug her claws in deeper, screeching in rage.

From the booth, Claire and the boys watched the battle. Gray mumbled to himself, calculating: "Seventy-eight . . . fifty-eight times two . . . a hundred ninety. We need more."

"More what?" Claire asked.

"Teeth," Gray said with great certainty. "We need more teeth."

Claire took this in. Then she took a deep breath,

grabbed a leather emergency pack from the wall, climbed out of the booth, and ran into the dark.

Blue and Charlie were down, leaving only Echo. A single raptor was no match for the *Indominus*. The massive dinosaur yanked Echo off her back, slammed her to the ground, and stomped her. She didn't get up.

As the *Indominus* stretched to her full height, Owen raced across the street and dove into the booth. He put Zach and Gray protectively behind him and looked around for Claire. "Where is she?"

Gray pointed outside. Owen rose to look in the direction he was pointing. *ROOAAARRR!* The *Indominus* jammed its head into the booth, snapping its jaws inches above them, rippling their clothes with the wind from its roaring mouth!

Chapter Twenty-Six

In a dark alley running alongside Main Street, Claire approached the huge steel door of a massive paddock. She pulled out her phone. "Lowery! Lowery! Are you still there?"

Lowery answered the call in the empty control room. "Claire! Where are you?"

"I need you to open Paddock Nine."

"*Nine?* Are you kidding?"

"Lowery, be a man and do something for once!"

Lowery looked hurt. "Why do you have to make it personal?" He turned to his keyboard, steeling himself. He typed, hesitated, and hit ENTER.

The massive steel door rose. Claire took a flare out of the emergency pouch and cracked it, lighting up the night.

BOOM. BOOM.

Footsteps thundered. Puddles rippled. When the

beast in the paddock drew dangerously near, Claire turned and ran back toward Main Street, holding the shining flare out behind her.

The *T. rex* passed through the open door, chasing the light.

The *Indominus* thrust her head deeper into the steel booth, unable to get her jaws around Owen and the boys. Claire ran onto Main Street and threw the lit flare at the *Indominus.*

SMASH! The *T. rex* crashed onto Main Street, knocking over a dinosaur sculpture. The *Indominus* pulled its head out of the booth and turned to face the *T. rex.*

For a moment, the two colossal beasts stood at opposite ends of the street, staring. Then they roared and rushed at each other, grappling, snapping their jaws, flailing their claws, and whipping their tails.

Claire tried to get back to the merchandise booth, but a gigantic tail swept her aside. She fell, hurt. Owen ran out and picked her up. He carried her back to the booth, dodging the two titanic combatants, just barely making it back safely.

Suddenly Blue reappeared out of the dark. She latched

her razor-sharp teeth onto the *Indominus*'s leg. As the *Indominus* turned its attention to Blue, the *T. rex* rose and slammed its head into the monster, which flew back into a concrete building, denting it. The *Indominus* fell onto the lagoon boardwalk with a thunderous crash. Blue and the *T. rex* roared together, united by an unnatural common enemy.

The *Indominus* struggled to her feet and roared back at them, lowering into a fighting stance. Suddenly— *ROOAARRRWWRR!* The *Mosasaurus* erupted out of the lagoon, clamped its huge jaws on the mighty *Indominus rex,* and dragged her into the water, deep below the surface.

The churning water slowly calmed. The *Indominus* did not emerge.

The *T. rex* snarled. It was weakened by injuries, but victorious. The *T. rex* and Blue looked at each other, unsure whether to fight. The *T. rex* turned away, choosing not to. Blue gave Owen a farewell glance, then disappeared into the shadows.

The *T. rex* looked up at the moon and lumbered off into the night, free to roam the island.

Zach and Gray's parents entered the school gym in

Costa Rica. It had been set up as an evacuation center. They saw a thousand people wrapped in Red Cross blankets eating donated food on paper plates. They scanned the crowd, searching anxiously for their children.

Mom saw a face she recognized: Claire's. Her sister was wrapped in a blanket.

Claire gave her sister a tearful smile, asking for forgiveness in a single look. She moved out of the way to reveal Zach and Gray seated on a cot. The parents ran to their sons.

They hugged Gray tight. Then they were completely surprised when their teenage son stepped forward and also hugged them, holding on.

Claire kept her distance, letting the family have its reunion. But then her sister walked over to her and pulled her close. Claire smiled through her tears, overwhelmed.

Through the sea of people, Claire spotted Owen in the doorway. He gave her a subtle tip of his cap. She hurried over to him.

"Looks like we're off our island," Claire said.

"Yeah, it does," he agreed.

"So what do we do now?" she asked.

"Probably stick together, at first, for survival."

She smiled, and they walked off together.

On Isla Nublar, Jurassic World was abandoned. It was a ghost town headed for extinction. A small flock of *Pteranodons* circled in the sky over the island.

On the roof of the visitors' center, the *T. rex* stood on the helipad, overlooking its dying kingdom. The king of the dinosaurs stood its ground and roared, ready to take on anything the modern world threw at it.